Jasper and th

Deirdre Madden's novels include *The Birds of the Innocent Wood*, *Nothing is Black*, *One by One in the Darkness*, and *Authenticity*. She has twice been shortlisted for the Orange Prize, most recently for *Molly Fox's Birthday*. She has also published three novels for children.

She teaches at Trinity College, Dublin, and is a member of the Irish Arts Academy Aosdána.

by the same author

FOR CHILDREN
Snakes' Elbows
Thanks for Telling Me, Emily

FOR ADULTS
Hidden Symptoms
Remembering Light and Stone
Nothing is Black
Authenticity
One by One in the Darkness
The Birds of the Innocent Wood
Molly Fox's Birthday

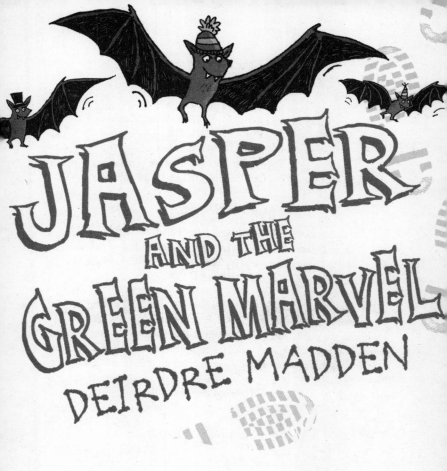

JASPER
AND THE
GREEN MARVEL

DEIRDRE MADDEN

ff

faber and faber

First published in 2012 by
Faber and Faber Limited
Bloomsbury House, 74–77 Great Russell Street,
London, WC1B 3DA

Typeset by Faber and Faber
Printed and bound by CPI Group (UK) Ltd, Croydon, CR0 4YY

A CIP record for this book
is available from the British Library

ISBN 978–0–571–26007–2

2 4 6 8 10 9 7 5 3 1

For Lara Marlowe, with love

Jasper Walks Free!

Just after dawn one fine summer morning the great door of Woodford prison swung open. A prison warder stuck his head out and had a good look around. 'There's no one there,' he said turning back into the prison. 'You can go out now.'

A tall man with a big black beard and carrying a suitcase stepped out into the morning light. 'Now then, Jasper,' said the prison officer, 'are you going to be a good boy from now on?' Jasper nodded. 'Promise?'

'Promise.' But Jasper had his fingers crossed behind his back when he said this, so perhaps he didn't mean it.

How Jasper Jellit came to be in Woodford prison in the first place is such an extraordinary story that you could write a book about it. In fact I've already done just that. The book is called *Snakes' Elbows*, and if you've read it you will know what a bad lad Jasper is. If you haven't read it, don't worry, you'll still be able to follow this new story with no trouble at all.

The prison officer handed Jasper a paper bag and an envelope. 'Here's some money to get you started and a couple of sandwiches. Goodbye! Good luck!'

'Good riddance!' Jasper said, as the door of the prison closed behind him, leaving him standing there alone on the step. He immediately opened the envelope and counted the banknotes it contained. 'What a swizz! Talk about mean! I'll have that spent in no time.' Then he looked into the paper bag. 'Oh no! Yuk! Egg and onion! Double yuk! I'm not eating that!' He threw the paper bag high in the air, back over the prison wall. 'Keep your manky sarnies!' he cried. 'I'm going to have a proper breakfast.'

And then Jasper did something very odd indeed. He opened his jacket and spoke to his inside pocket. 'Are you going to be good boys? Are you going to behave yourselves?' Two little heads popped up from inside the pocket, with whiskered snouts and beady bright eyes. This was Toe-Rag and Scum-Bag and they were *rats*. Jasper had made pets of them while he was in prison and decided to take them with him when he left. You'll be glad to hear that over the years their horrible names had been shortened to Rags and Bags. 'Well then, I'm waiting. Are you going to be good?'

The two rats nodded, but deep in the pocket they had their claws crossed behind their backs, so perhaps, like Jasper, they didn't really mean it either. They were annoyed with him for having thrown away the sandwiches. Rags and Bags would have eaten them, but then again, they'd have eaten anything. Can you imagine the stink of a rat that's just had an egg and onion sandwich? You can hardly blame Jasper for not wanting to have a couple of creatures like that in his pocket.

Closing over his jacket again, Jasper picked up his suitcase and walked off through the silent empty streets of the little town in search of breakfast.

2

Breakfast

He pushed open the door of the first café he came to and was met by the rich tempting smell of fried food. He sat down at a table and the waitress came over to him. She wore a dirty apron covered in greasy stains and had a tiny net hat balanced on top of her curly hair.

'What d'you want?'

'What d'you have?'

'Sausages an' rashers an' baked beans an' mushrooms an' fried eggs an' fried potatoes an' fried tomatoes an' fried bread,' said the waitress.

'I'll take the lot!' cried Jasper. 'With toast and a big pot of tea.'

'Magic word?' the woman said.

'Please,' replied Jasper in a sulky voice.

Before long he was tucking into a monster fry-up, with a shiny brown pot of tea and a great hot haystack of buttered toast. From time to time he slipped the odd bit of food into his jacket pocket: a bacon rind, a crust or two, the end of a sausage. Over the years Jasper had become very skilful at sneaking food to the rats in this way. You could have been sitting right in front of him and you wouldn't have seen him doing it; he was like a magician.

But Bags and Rags were annoyed because he wasn't giving them anything like as much food as they wanted. All their lives they had known nothing but prison grub, porridge, and dry bread and hard biscuits. Compared to that, the little tasty-bites they were getting this morning were so yummy! They wanted more.

After he had finished eating, Jasper poured himself a fourth cup of tea and started to think about what he was going to do. When he went into prison he had lost everything. The money in the envelope wasn't going to last very long. He was going to have to find a place to live and he was going to have to find a job and all of this was going to be a great big problem. Jasper loved luxury and the best of everything, but he hated having to work. He picked up a copy of the local newspaper, the *Woodford Trumpet*, from a nearby table and turned to the pages where the jobs were advertised.

These are the kind of things he was hoping to find there:

WANTED

SOFA TESTER

Must be very lazy and good at doing nothing for hours on end.

Excellent pay

No experience necessary

Apply to: Sofas 4 U, Woodford.

We are looking for an assistant to the chef in our

FIVE STAR RESTAURANT

The successful candidate will be required to eat lunch

and dinner every day and then tell the chef whether

or not he's any good at his job.

This is what he actually found:

INCREDIBLY HARD WORKER WANTED
TO DIG HOLES IN THE ROAD
WHATEVER THE WEATHER.
MUST HAVE OWN SHOVEL.
THE HARDER YOU DIG . . .
. . . THE MORE YOU EARN!

Washer-upper
wanted for busy hotel.
Must be prepared to start early,
finish late, and work all weekend.
No sense of smell an advantage.

8

There were other jobs too but they all seemed to offer long hours, hard dull work and measly wages. Jasper didn't like the look of this at all. He called to the waitress to bring him a fresh pot of tea, and as he turned back to the newspaper he saw an advertisement that he hadn't noticed earlier.

---

*Gardener wanted for
Haverford-Snuffley Hall.
Live-in position.
Good salary. All meals provided.
Must like bats!*

*Apply to Mrs Haverford-Snuffley,
Haverford-Snuffley Hall, Woodford.*

Jasper knew who Mrs Haverford-Snuffley was. She had been an important part of the whole adventure that had led to his being in prison in the first place. He studied the newspaper carefully.

The thing that appealed to him most in the advertisement was the 'live-in' bit. Haverford-Snuffley Hall was a gorgeous house, almost as nice as the place in which Jasper himself had once lived. He liked the sound of the good pay and the meals as well. He couldn't stand bats – nasty black things with their wings and their horrible pointed teeth. Ugh, he thought, they were so creepy! But he could always pretend to like them. Mrs Haverford-Snuffley was a daft old coot, it would be easy to fool her. He didn't much like the thought of gardening but it couldn't be that difficult, could it? Even if you didn't bother to do anything at all to them, flowers and trees kept on growing, didn't they? Mrs Haverford-Snuffley wouldn't be able to follow him around the garden, she would be too busy looking after her wretched bats. He could sit and read a newspaper in the greenhouse when he was supposed to be doing the tomatoes, or he might be able to snooze in the potting shed.

He was still thinking about all of this when the waitress came back with a fresh pot of tea.

The Waitress's Granny

The waitress set the teapot on the table and then, much to Jasper's annoyance, she plonked herself down in a chair beside him. 'Haverford-Snuffley Hall!' she said, noticing where Jasper had the paper folded open at the advertisement. 'Now that's a place I haven't been to for years. Oooh, that brings back such memories! When I was a nipper I used to go there every single Sunday afternoon to visit my granny.'

'Your granny?' said Jasper? 'Your granny used to live in Haverford-Snuffley Hall?' The woman nodded. Jasper was impressed, because on top of everything else, he was a ferocious snob.

'She was a laundry maid. Live-in, you see. Oh, there was never anybody like Granny with the old soap and starch. Famous for it, she was,' the woman said dreamily. 'There was no stain she couldn't get out; her whites would have dazzled your eyes. There was no other laundry maid who could get a tablecloth or an apron as crisp and white as Granny could.'

What would your granny say if she could see you now? Jasper thought, gazing sourly at the waitress's greasy pinny, with its egg and ketchup stains. Do you think she'd be proud of you? You're not exactly following in the family tradition.

'What were the gardens at Haverford-Snuffley Hall like then?' he asked aloud, and his heart sank when the woman said, 'Immense. They seemed to me to go on forever. Orchards and a walled garden, a kitchen garden full of vegetables and soft fruit, glass houses, shrubberies and more flower beds than you ever could count. And everything was kept to the pitch of perfection: not so much as a daisy on the lawn, not a single petal or leaf out of place.' Jasper listened to her in dismay. 'The house had got a bit crumbly in recent years, but it was done up a while back.' Yes, Jasper knew that it had been done up.

'The thing Granny didn't like about being there was that the house was haunted.' Jasper gave a little snort of contempt at this – he didn't believe in ghosts, not for a minute. 'Oh, you can scoff,' the waitress said, 'but it's the truth. Granny never actually saw a ghost there, but she heard it. It used to wake her up, moaning and wailing, in the middle of the night. What was really strange was that it wasn't just the house that was haunted, there was a ghost in the garden too.'

'And it wailed too, I suppose?' Jasper asked sarcastically.

'No,' the waitress admitted. 'It was very odd, it was musical. You'd be walking in the garden, Granny used to say, with not a bother on you, and the next thing you'd hear music coming from nowhere – the saddest music you can imagine. Oooh, it used to break her heart to hear it. She said that the wailing in the night frightened her out of her wits, but that the music was worse.'

'You'll be telling me next you can smell ghosts,' Jasper said. He was fed up now listening to this woman ramble on, and was just about to suggest that she go back to her grill-plate and frying pans when she said, 'There's hidden treasure in that house too. Well, there's supposed to be.'

'Treasure?' Jasper said. 'What kind of treasure?'

'An emerald necklace,' the woman said. 'It was known as the Green Marvel because all the jewels in it were so big, especially the central stone. It was just enormous.' Now Jasper was really interested.

'Hidden, you say?'

'Well, it's supposed to be lost somewhere in

the house. But maybe there was no such thing. You know the way people make up stories. I believe in the ghost, but I'm not sure that I believe in the Green Marvel.'

Jasper thought the exact opposite. He was convinced now that there were jewels hidden in Haverford–Snuffley Hall, but he didn't believe for a moment that there were ghosts. The gardening job was beginning to look most attractive to him.

Just with that, the strangest thing happened. The woman's face went a funny purple colour and she jumped up on to her chair. She opened her mouth wide and she screamed. 'AAAARRRGH!'

What's got into her all of a sudden? Jasper wondered. She pulled her pinny up over her head and stood on one leg, then she screamed again. 'AAAAARGH! RATS! AAAAARGH!'

There on the table, as bold as you like, were Rags and Bags! Jasper had been so busy listening to the woman's stories about

Haverford-Snuffley Hall and the Green Marvel that he had forgotten all about them. The rats had sneaked out of his pocket and had eaten all the leftovers on the table, all the rinds and crusts. By the time the waitress noticed them, Rags was tucking into the sugar lumps in the china sugar bowl, and Bags had his head deep in the milk jug. The woman screamed one last time and then she fainted out cold, falling off the chair and on to the floor.

'What did I say to you two about behaving yourselves?' Jasper bellowed. 'What did I say about being good? Get in here now!' He held his jacket open and the two rats quickly slunk back into the inside pocket. Jasper fastened his buttons so that they wouldn't be able to get out again without his noticing. The woman gave a little moan. She was coming round. Quick as a flash Jasper picked up his suitcase and ran out of the café.

He raced off down the street, ran and ran through the little town until he was completely out of puff, by which stage he was at the edge of Woodford, where the fields and the farms began. Stopping to catch his breath, he reflected that things had turned out rather well after all. He had had a jolly good breakfast and he hadn't had to pay a penny for it. He still had all the money the prison officer had given him safe in the envelope. Opposite where he was standing he could see a signpost, hidden in the hedge. He moved the branches aside and read:

'HAVERFORD-SNUFFLEY HALL 4 MILES'

There was a painted hand pointing in the right direction.

That'll be a long walk, he thought, and then a hay cart appeared. Jasper waited until it had passed and then he ran behind it. He tossed his suitcase up on the hay, then he took a flying leap and jumped on himself.

'Well done me!' he crowed. 'First a free breakfast and now a free ride to where I'm going.' He unbuttoned his jacket and the two rats popped out of his pocket. Jasper was too cheerful now to be cross with them any longer. 'Everything's going our way, lads,' he cried. 'Everything's going to be fine!' The two rats bounced up and down on the hay with delight. The sunlight sparkled down through the trees as the cart trundled along the country road, taking Jasper to his destination: Haverford-Snuffley Hall.

At Haverford-Snuffley Hall

The hay cart seemed to Jasper to be going slowly, but when he got to his destination and tried to get down from it, it appeared to be going very fast indeed. Just as he had jumped on to it, there now seemed nothing for it but to jump off. 'One, two three . . .' *Crump!* And he landed on his back in the dusty road, with his suitcase beside him and the two rats sitting on his head. They at least had made sure of a soft landing. He struggled to his feet and limped through the gates of Haverford-Snuffley Hall, which were marked by two big pillars with a stone dragon sitting on top of each one. He walked up the driveway but as he came within sight of the house something rather strange happened.

He could see Haverford–Snuffley Hall there before him but it was green. The door was green and the windows were green, even the walls and the roof appeared green to him. This was because Jasper was seeing the place through a haze of envy. The house might well have been called 'Thisreallyshouldbemyplace Hall' or 'Snotfairthatitisntmine Court' as far as Jasper was concerned. Once he had had a house every bit as special as this and it filled him with rage to think that he had lost it. But then he told himself he would have to try to hide his feelings. He would have to try to be charming and friendly. He blinked hard twice and the house now looked to him as it really was.

Haverford–Snuffley Hall was a big, square, peach–coloured house with white window frames and a flowering plant growing up a trellis beside the front door. It sat in the middle of spectacular gardens – immense, as the waitress had remarked, with every kind of tree and flower you could imagine. As Jasper approached, he noticed an elderly lady sitting on a wooden chair by the front step, reading a book. She had grey hair and a sweet-natured face. Her clothes were quite unremarkable but for one detail. She was wearing a straw hat with a long brown feather in it and from the end of this feather dangled a tiny bat. Stranger still, the bat was also wearing a hat: a little pale bonnet tied firmly under its chin with a green ribbon so that it wouldn't fall off, for the bat was hanging upside down, as bats do.

Jasper knew that this was Mrs Haverford-Snuffley because he had met her in the past. She, however, did not recognise Jasper, because of the big black beard he had grown in prison, and he was happy about this.

'Good morning, young man,' she said politely. 'How may I help you?'

'Why no, madam,' said Jasper gallantly,

flashing a brilliant smile at her. 'The question is this: how may *I* help *you*? A little bird told me that you were looking for a gardener, and I believe myself to be just the man for the job.'

'Don't tell me!' she cried, clapping her hands and closing her eyes. 'You're an expert! You've studied plants and flowers for years! You have a degree in horticulture! You have years of experience both here and abroad in some of the most remarkable gardens in the world! I knew it! Don't tell me! I knew it!'

Jasper was glad that he didn't have to tell her. It was what he wanted her to believe, and yet nothing could have been further from the truth. He knew absolutely nothing about gardens and flowers. He was aware of the little bat staring coldly at him. Jasper stared back. 'Do please tell me, sir, what is your name?'

Now this was a tricky one. If he said 'Jasper Jellit' she would most likely scream and run into the house and perhaps send someone out to chase him away, because everyone in

Woodford knew that Jasper Jellit was a villain of the first order. He had given no thought to a new name before he came up to the house. 'My name?' he said. 'My name, sweet lady? Might I humbly suggest . . .' and he looked around at the flowers of the garden '. . . might I ask you to be good enough to call me . . . Professor Orchid?'

'How wonderful!' cried Mrs Haverford-Snuffley. 'Professor! As soon as I saw you I knew that you were a learned man.' Jasper smiled. Wasn't that clever of me? he said to himself. Clever as well to borrow my new name from that flower growing right beside the door! Quick thinking or what? Of course, what Jasper took to be an orchid was nothing of the kind: it was actually a honeysuckle. You see, he really did know nothing whatsoever about gardening.

'You do know that it's a live-in position?' Mrs Haverford-Snuffley said and Jasper sighed.

'I do indeed, madam. I must tell you that

it will grieve me greatly not to be in my own dear home but one must make sacrifices for excellence, must one not?'

'Well, given your remarkable qualifications, Professor Orchid,' she said timidly, 'perhaps in your case I must make an exception. It seems unreasonable to expect a man like you to be away from his own house – indeed, away from his own garden. So as a special favour to you, we can forget about the live-in bit.'

'No!' Jasper almost screamed at her, suddenly terrified that the chance he had would slip through his fingers. That was the whole point of the job: to live in. He had nowhere else to go. 'No, madam, I insist! I will live under your roof. Such is my dedication that your garden will become the centre of my life and it would pain me to be far from your flowers. How could I sleep at night, knowing that I was miles from your hyacinths? I would toss and turn in my bed, worrying that your lobelia might need me and I was nowhere to be found. No, madam,' he said again, this time quite sternly, 'we will discuss it no further. I will live in Haverford-Snuffley Hall and that's the end of it.'

'Never did I think to find such dedication!' she sighed. Suddenly the little bat began to bounce up and down on the end of the feather to get her attention. 'Oh, how could I have forgotten!' said Mrs Haverford-Snuffley. 'There is one last question, Professor Orchid, and it is the most important of all: do you like bats?'

'Like them?' said Jasper. 'Why I LOVE them! Of all the creatures on the earth they're my number-one favourite.'

'I'm so relieved to hear it. No matter how good a gardener you were, no matter how much of an expert, it simply wouldn't do if you didn't like bats. But then I can never understand how there could be anybody who wouldn't like them.' She rolled her eyes to look at the little dark animal that was bouncing gently just beside her head. 'Isn't that true, my poppet? Who wouldn't love Mummy's dear little batty-watty? Who's a cutie-pie little fly-by-night, eh? Who's the best bat in the whole wide world?' Suddenly she stopped. 'What's that strange noise, Professor Orchid? Can you hear it? A kind of squeaking sound. Do you know what it is?'

Jasper knew exactly what it was. It was the sound of the two rats in his inside pocket, laughing themselves silly at all the bat baby-talk. 'Indigestion. Do please excuse me, madam,' he murmured and he smacked his jacket hard with the flat of his hand. The squeaking stopped.

'Perhaps you're hungry,' she said. 'Let me show you to your room and then I'll get the cook to send you up some tea and scones. Oh, I'm so glad you're going to be working here! Welcome to Haverford-Snuffley Hall, Professor Orchid.'

'The pleasure,' Jasper said smoothly, picking up his suitcase to follow her, 'the pleasure, madam, is all mine.'

Meet Mrs Knuttmegg

The room to which Mrs Haverford-Snuffley showed Jasper had a nice brass bed and a little fireplace. The wallpaper was patterned with ivy and roses. 'You'll love this,' Mrs Haverford-Snuffley cried, drawing back the curtains. 'A view of the kitchen gardens!'

Jasper forced a smile. The room wasn't anything like as grand as he had hoped or imagined. He would have liked to have a whole floor of the house all to himself, or at the very least a suite of rooms. He had expected a view of rolling lawns, of fountains and shrubberies and what did he get instead? A few measly rows of leeks and cabbages. 'Very nice,' he said through gritted teeth. It wasn't at all what he wanted but it would have to do.

'Put your suitcase down and come with me,' said Mrs Haverford-Snuffley. 'There's someone I want you to meet.' She took Jasper downstairs again, not by the wide sweeping curved staircase by which they had come up, but by a narrow flight of wooden steps directly outside his bedroom door. This mean little staircase ended in a stone-flagged hallway, where there was a wooden door. 'Coo-eee!' she cried, pushing the door open. 'It's only me! Are you there, Mrs Knuttmegg?'

Jasper found himself in a kitchen where a woman was standing baking at a table, up to her elbows in flour. Unlike the waitress in the café, she wore a spotless crisp white apron.

'Mrs Knuttmegg, meet Professor Orchid, our new gardener! Professor Orchid, this is Mrs Knuttmegg, my wonderful, wonderful cook.'

There were three types of people that Jasper

didn't like and didn't trust in life: baldy barbers, laughing policemen and skinny cooks. Mrs Knuttmegg was the thinnest cook you could imagine. She looked at Jasper closely.

'So you're the new gardener fellow, eh? Like your grub then, do you?'

'I do indeed,' he replied, flashing her a smile. 'I'm something of a gourmet, if I may say so. I like my fish grilled rather than poached. I can only eat carrots if they're cut into little sticks. I simply can't touch them when they've been cut into circles. If I have parsnips they have to be cubed and if I have peas then I absolutely must have creamed potatoes as well. I can stick the peas together with the potato and then they don't roll off the fork and when I have sausages . . .'

'HA!' Mrs Knuttmegg interrupted him with a loud hoot of mirthless laughter and then went on with her baking.

'What are you making?' Mrs Haverford-Snuffley asked. 'Something scrumptious?'

'Scones,' said Mrs Knuttmegg. 'Cherry ones.' Jasper would have preferred to have sultanas but he thought it might not be a good idea to say so.

'Ooh, yummy-wummy! My favourites!'

'I'll send some up to you in the drawing room, missus, as soon as they're ready, with tea and some of that nice blackcurrant jam I have.'

'Thank you so much, Mrs Knuttmegg. Would you be so kind as to send some up to Professor Orchid too?'

'I will indeed,' she replied. 'There'll be scones especially for you, mister.'

Jasper would have been happier about this had it not been for the sly smile she gave him as she said it.

'Might I now meet the butler?' Jasper asked. 'The housemaids and the boot-boy?' The two women looked at each other and then they both burst out laughing. 'I'm afraid there are no such people,' Mrs Haverford-Snuffley said.

'You and Mrs Knuttmegg form my entire household.'

'I'm the housekeeper as well as the cook. And I hope you're good at odd jobs as well as gardening, cos there'll be plenty of those to do.'

Jasper was furious to learn this, and he'd had enough of this nasty, skinny, spiteful woman. He turned away and said haughtily 'You can bring my scones up to me when they're ready, and I'll have coffee rather than tea.'

'In your dreams, mister! I've more to do than to run up and down stairs to wait on you. Didn't you notice one of those things in your room?' She nodded across the kitchen towards two small steel doors set in the wall.

'It's a dumb-waiter,' Mrs Haverford-Snuffley said helpfully. She pressed a button and the doors opened. 'It's like a tiny lift, you see, Professor Orchid. Mrs Knuttmegg puts the food in it and then she can send it up to me or to you. It's an awfully clever idea, isn't it?' Jasper didn't reply. Mrs Knuttmegg tipped her scone dough out on to the floury table. 'We must leave you to your work,' Mrs Haverford-Snuffley said.

'Just one minute, missus.' Mrs Knuttmegg picked up a cherry. 'Here you are, possum,' she said. Leaning over, she popped it into the bat's mouth.

'How kind! You like a fruity treat, don't you, sweetie?' Mrs Haverford-Snuffley cried. 'A nice fat cherry-werry for the batty-watty!'

Jasper could hear the two rats in his pocket laughing again.

6

Jasper Settles In

Back up in his room, Jasper locked the door and started to unpack. He took the two rats out of his pocket and let them scamper about the place. Rags and Bags had spent all of their lives in prison and they weren't in the least bit disappointed with Haverford-Snuffley Hall. Jasper's room, with its flowery wallpaper and brass bed, was the height of luxury as far as they were concerned.

Jasper was just hanging the last of his clothes in the wardrobe when *PING!* The steel doors of the dumb-waiter opened.

'Oh no!'

Inside there was a pot of tea, a cup and a plate with four cherry scones. But the scones were tiny! Never in all his life had Jasper seen such teeny-tiny scones. ''Snot fair!' he shouted. 'And I said I didn't want tea, I want coffee!'

Suddenly something outrageous happened. The two rats leapt into the dumb-waiter and scoffed the four scones as quick as a wink: two each! Jasper couldn't believe what he was seeing and he screeched in rage. Then he reached into the dumb-waiter and hauled Rags and Bags out by the tails.

'Now you listen to me!' he roared holding them upside down. 'What did I say outside the prison? What did I say about being good?'

The rats sniggered and licked the last sweet crumbs off their snouts. They didn't care a hoot what Jasper said. A fry-up and sugar-cubes for breakfast and now a snack of perfectly rat-sized scones mid-morning: nothing, but nothing was going to spoil their day.

Jasper opened his empty suitcase and

dropped the two rats into it, slammed it closed and locked it. 'I'll show you who's boss. You'll stay there as a punishment until I let you out.'

Still Rags and Bags didn't care. They were tired after their early start and all the excitement, and in no time at all they were both fast asleep with their tails curled around their back paws.

Jasper spent the rest of the morning wandering around Haverford–Snuffley Hall looking at all the portraits in gold frames, at the silver and the furniture. He thought how unfair it was that everything he saw belonged to a daft old coot with a bat hanging off her hat instead of belonging to him.

In the afternoon, Mrs Haverford–Snuffley took him round the garden to show him where he would be working. It took ages because it was extremely big, and before long Jasper was so bored he thought he would weep. It was hard work too, because he had to pretend to be an expert. Although she didn't know it,

Mrs Haverford-Snuffley knew far more about flowers and plants than he did. Jasper couldn't tell his begonias from his Busy Lizzies, much less his nasturtiums from his narcissi. She would stand in front of a flower bed and say, 'Now my gladioli are doing exceptionally well this year,' and Jasper would agree and nod his head, hoping that he was looking at the right thing.

Late that night, up in his room, he let the rats out of the suitcase. He opened the top drawer of the dressing table and popped Rags and Bags into it. Then he took off his socks and gave the rats one each. They wriggled into them as if the socks were sleeping bags, pulled them up around themselves until only their heads were sticking out. Jasper took off his vest and rolled it up as a pillow for them. The vest was sweaty and manky but it was nothing compared to the socks. The rats liked it that way; they liked their bedding smelly and vile.

'Night-night, lads,' Jasper said. 'Sweet dreams. And remember what I said: be good.' In no time at all he was asleep and snoring, but Rags and Bags were wide awake and excited. Having slept all day in the suitcase they weren't in the least bit tired.

'Come on, Rags,' Bags said, peeling off his sock sleeping-bag. 'Let's go and have some fun! Let's explore our new home!'

Rags and Bags Go Exploring

Rags and Bags climbed on to the table that stood conveniently near to the dumb-waiter, and Bags pushed the button on the wall. They were afraid that the loud *PING!* it made might wake Jasper but he went on snoring as the metal doors opened. Rags hopped in and then Bags pushed the button again. He just about managed to jump nimbly into the dumb-waiter beside Rags before the doors closed, almost nipping his tail.

Down, down, down went the dumb-waiter. 'Hang on,' Rags said suddenly. 'What if we need someone on the outside to push the button to let us out? What if we get stuck in here?' It was a terrible thought. They imagined having to stay there all night until Mrs Knuttmegg opened the dumb-waiter in the morning to send Jasper up his breakfast. Then they would really be in trouble – big trouble.

It was an enormous relief therefore when the dumb-waiter came to a stop and the doors opened immediately. The two rats scampered out into a silent and deserted kitchen, where a single small lamp burned. What a delightful place it was! The heat of the stove made it cosy and snug and the air was full of delicious smells which the rats couldn't recognise, but which made their mouths water.

On the kitchen table there was a pile of cherry scones on a plate left over from that morning, but unfortunately for Rags and Bags they were covered with a heavy glass dome. Try as the two rats might, they couldn't get it shifted. They pushed hard and then they pulled even harder. They wound their tails around the knob on top of the dome and tried to drag the thing over but it wouldn't budge. It was really irritating because they so wanted to get at the scones. When they finally gave up they felt foolish to realise that sitting beside them, uncovered and there for the taking, was a bowl of stewed apples that they hadn't even noticed.

It took no time at all to eat every last little scrap of the apples, which were exceptionally tasty. Mrs Knuttmegg, who was an excellent cook, had added cinnamon and cloves and even a handful of raisins. Never could the rats have imagined that anything could be so delicious. It more than made up for not being able to get at the scones. When the bowl was empty they looked around, but there was nothing else to eat. No matter: their bellies were full and they were happy. 'Come on!' Bags said. 'Let's go and see what the rest of this house is like.'

There were two doors, one at each end of the kitchen. They knew that one opened on to the wooden staircase that led back up to

Jasper's room and they didn't want that, and so they slipped through the other door. There was a long corridor, a flight of steps going up and then another door and then behind that . . .

What wonders met their eyes! Haverford-Snuffley Hall dazzled the two rats. They tiptoed down corridors where their feet sank deep into soft carpet, right up to their tummies. They crossed wooden floors so highly polished that they could see their own faces reflected back to them. High above them on the walls were beautiful paintings in golden frames, and the walls themselves were covered in silk, yellow and green and pale blue. In prison everything had been ugly and grey; here even the least little thing was special and bright.

They must have spent hours going from room to room, until at last they ended up in the front hall of the house, where there was a huge mirror and a curved, sweeping staircase made of white wood. They were just beginning to think that perhaps they should make their way back to Jasper's room and climb into their socks again when suddenly, just above their heads, someone spoke.

'Who are you?' asked a little voice.

8

Nelly

It was the tiny bat that usually hung from the feather on Mrs Haverford-Snuffley's hat, but tonight it was hanging from the edge of a small table. It was upside down and was still wearing its own little bonnet, tied under its chin with a green ribbon.

'Hello!' Bags cried. 'What's your name then?'

'Nelly,' said the bat, and then it said again, 'Who are you?'

'That's for us to know and for you to wonder,' Rags said. 'Snooky-ookums! Mummy's little batty-watty! What are you doing here anyway?'

'I'm going home,' the bat said in a sulky voice.

'What d'you mean, home? Don't you live here?' But before the bat could explain to Rags, Bags had jumped up and pulled Nelly's bonnet off.

'Stop that! That's not fair!' she cried, as the rat put the bonnet on its own head, letting the ribbons dangle. 'I'm telling! Give it back to me!'

'Diddy-widdy-snooky-wooky! Mummy's baby-waby! *I'm telling! Give it back to me*!' And Bags teased the bat, imitating it in a high, silly voice while Rags cackled with nasty laughter.

'Give me my bonnet! I am going to tell on you!' Nelly was struggling hard not to cry, as the rats took it in turn to try on her hat. They minced up and down the tiled floor of the hall, sniggering together and mocking her. When they were fed up with that, they threw the bonnet back. Nelly caught it and tied it on to her head immediately.

'Who are you going to tell?' they sneered.

'Wouldn't you like to know?' Nelly replied coldly and there was something in her tone as she said it that worried them slightly.

'Mrs Haverford-Snuffley?' they asked and she shook her head.

'Who, then?' But she didn't reply, and said instead, 'You'll be sorry you did this. REALLY sorry.' And then Nelly did something that absolutely astonished them.

She flew away!

Strange as it may seem, the rats hadn't even noticed until then that Nelly had wings. When she was hanging from Mrs Haverford-Snuffley's hat she always kept them neatly folded against her sides, and so it was a tremendous shock to them when she took off into juddering flight from the edge of the table. She flew high up and circled the chandelier twice on her wide, ribbed black wings, then cried again, 'You'll be really sorry! I am going to tell!' before disappearing off up the hallway, into the darkness of the sleeping house.

The two rats stared after her. What a night! And now it was almost over, because through the hall window they could see the first faint traces of dawn in the sky. 'We'd better get back to the room before Jasper wakes up.'

It was easier said than done. They had wandered all over the house in the course of the night and although they thought they knew the way back, they quickly got lost. They trudged up and down for ages, arguing, blaming each other, both tired by now and beginning to get hungry again. It was a great relief when they finally found Jasper's room. He was still snoring loudly in his brass bed as they crept back into their sock sleeping-bags, ready to nod off themselves, for they were worn out after all their adventures.

But to their dismay no sooner had they put their heads on the rolled-up vest and were about to drift off when Jasper's alarm clock went off with a loud jangle of bells. Oh no!

'Morning, lads! Shake a leg! Wakey-wakey!'

9

The Green Marvel

As Jasper was leaving the house to begin his first day's work, he bumped into Mrs Knuttmegg at the bottom of the wooden stairs, and she glared at him.

'Hungry during the night then, were you?' she barked.

'Yes, I was actually,' Jasper replied. The dinner she had sent up to him the previous evening hadn't been as mean and mingy as the scones, but it hadn't been a particularly generous helping either. 'I was very hungry indeed.'

Mrs Knuttmegg seemed astonished by this. 'Well, you're a cheeky fellow and no mistake.'

And then she announced, for no reason that Jasper could see, 'There's nothing Mrs Haverford-Snuffley likes more for her breakfast than stewed apples with cloves, cinnamon and raisins.'

'Then why don't you cook some for her?' Jasper said. 'That's your job, isn't it?'

'You pup!' she cried. 'You cheeky pup! I'll let you away with it this time but you watch yourself, mister, because I'll be watching you. You mind your step.' And she stumped off back to her kitchen.

Let me away with it this time? Jasper wondered. Let me away with what? I haven't done anything. And that talk about stewed apples, what was that all about? The woman's clearly mad as well as nasty.

He went out into the sunny garden to start work. Mrs Haverford-Snuffley had suggested he begin by cutting the lawn, which he thought would be easy enough. And it was, in so far as all that was required was to push the mower up and down, stopping from time to time to empty the grass box into a barrow and then to wheel it away. The problem was that the lawns were so huge that it was tremendously hard work. Jasper pushed and cut and emptied and wheeled for hours and still he had made little progress.

Why didn't that woman buy one of those nifty mowers with an engine and a seat, he wondered as he emptied the grass box for the umpteenth time. Then I could zoom up and down and get the job done in no time at all. Lunchtime seemed to take forever to come, and the knowledge that the rats were snoozing in his pockets didn't improve his temper. Lazy creatures! They've got bone idle since we left prison. They're always sleeping these days.

At last noon came and he settled down to eat the packed lunch that Mrs Knuttmegg had sent up to him in the dumb-waiter that morning. There were cheese sandwiches made on white bread – the most boring sandwiches in the whole world as far as Jasper was concerned. Still, it could have been worse: at least they weren't egg and onion. There were a couple of apples too and a flask of tea – no chocolate biscuits, in fact no treats at all.

As he sat there glumly eating his dull lunch Jasper thought to himself, Things really aren't working out for me here the way I'd planned. I have to work hard, the food's rubbish and my room is nothing special. The cook's mad, she doesn't like me, and my boss is a lulu. Surely a smart chap like me can do far better than this. I should move on and try my luck again elsewhere.

Just with that, he saw Mrs Haverford-Snuffley approach from the far side of the garden, with the little bat bouncing on the end of the feather.

'Yoo-hoo! May I join you, Professor Orchid?'

Jasper smiled insincerely. 'Why of course, dear lady.' *Lulu-in-chief*, he thought, as she trotted across the lawn towards him. *Queen Lulu.*

As she drew near, he could see that she was carrying a baby fox in her arms and that one of its paws was bandaged up.

'Look at this poor little soldier, Professor Orchid. I found him down by the shrubbery. He's hurt his foot.'

'How heartbreaking,' said Jasper.

'Yes, isn't it?' she said, not hearing the sarcasm in his voice. 'But I've washed it and strapped it up for him.'

'So now what are you going to do with him?'

'I'll keep him in the house and look after him until he's well enough to go back into the wild.' She had settled herself beside Jasper on the bench and she cuddled the small fox to her.

'Do you know what my dream is, Professor? To open an animal sanctuary right here at Haverford-Snuffley Hall. I'd take in all kinds of creatures: pets, farm animals, wild animals, the lot. Pigs, kittens, hedgehogs, and our little foxy friends. Any animal in need of help or care or a new home would find a refuge here. It would be looked after until it was ready to be released back into the wild or to be settled with some kind people to begin a new life. I should like to help animals in this way more than anything else.'

'So why don't you do it?' Jasper asked. Mrs Haverford-Snuffley gave a huge sigh.

'Money, I'm afraid. It would take an absolute fortune. If I sold the house I could afford it, but then I would have nowhere to build the sanctuary. What I need is one single valuable thing that I could sell. For example, some years ago I had a very special painting and I was able to sell that to get the house fixed up. The place was in a dreadful state in those days, quite falling apart. So we got everything mended and improved and we also looked after my dear little batty-watty friends, didn't we, possum? We did! We did! We made the bats comfy and snug!'

Mrs Haverford-Snuffley stood up and

stroked the fox between its pointed ears. 'Yes, if only I had something of immense value to sell. It's at times like this that I wish I knew where the Green Marvel was. Ah well, we can dream, can't we? Anyway, I must stop chattering and let you get on with your work. Good afternoon, Professor Orchid!'

10

Mrs Haverford-Snuffley Explains

At the words 'the Green Marvel,' Jasper almost fell off the bench.

'What? Stop! No! Wait! Help!'

Mrs Haverford-Snuffley, who had been walking away, turned back to him, her pale blue eyes full of astonishment. 'What is it, Professor?'

'It's just – why, it's nothing – it's – I – you mentioned the Green Marvel,' he stammered. 'Won't you tell me about it, please?'

'Haven't you heard of it already? I thought it was famous in Woodford. It's certainly a legend here in Haverford-Snuffley Hall. Come with me and I'll show you.'

Still carrying the little fox in her arms she led Jasper across the lawns to the house and together they went into the hallway, where she stopped in front of a painting.

'There, Professor Orchid,' she said. 'That's the Green Marvel for you.'

The painting was a life-size portrait of a pretty woman with curly dark red hair, not unlike the colour of the fox, piled on top of her head. She had pale skin and a beautiful straight nose. Her flowing gown was made of dark blue silk and she carried a fan made of soft feathers. Did Jasper notice any of this? I doubt it, which is odd, because usually he was very fond of looking at pretty girls. But the only thing that interested him in this painting was the necklace that the young woman was wearing.

It was a truly extraordinary necklace made of emeralds: radiant deep green stones. There were square jewels and some were cut into the shape of a pear and these hung from the necklace itself. 'Do you see that enormous rectangular stone right in the middle, Professor? It's believed to be the biggest emerald ever found.'

Yes, Jasper saw it and he could well believe that what Mrs Haverford–Snuffley said was true. Even he couldn't imagine a bigger emerald. He stood there looking at the painting with his mouth hanging open, overcome with terrible feelings of greed and desire. So this was the Green Marvel.

Jasper wanted it.

'Where is it now?' he said when he was at last able to speak again.

'That's the problem, nobody knows. It belonged to Georgiana Haverford–Snuffley, the girl in the painting. She was the daughter of Theophilus Haverford–Snuffley. He was very fond of pictures and it was he who had the Haverford–Snuffley Angel painted more than two hundred years ago – but that's a whole other story.'

'Indeed,' said Jasper, who knew more than enough about the Haverford-Snuffley Angel.

'The story goes,' she continued, 'that the Green Marvel is hidden somewhere here in the Hall. When I was little I remember hearing it said that it was hidden in the kitchen, but that can't be true, or I'm sure Mrs Knuttmegg would have come across it long before now. Nobody knows for sure, maybe it's gone for good. Maybe it was stolen or simply lost. But, who knows, Professor, you might even find it when you're out digging.' For a moment Jasper was tempted to run outside and grab his shovel, and to dig and dig and dig.

'I'm joking, of course, it's highly unlikely that that will happen. But the story is quite persistent that it was hidden here and has never been found. If only I knew where it was! Then my little foxy-woxy and all his friends could live happily ever after, couldn't you, my love? I'd take care of you.'

And you would too, you mad old cabbage

of a lulu, Jasper thought angrily. You'd use it to help a bunch of mangy, good-for-nothing animals.

In that moment his mind was quite made up. He decided that he wasn't going to leave, no matter how much he hated the food and the work. He would stay in Haverford-Snuffley Hall, he would find the Green Marvel and he would keep it for himself!

But what Jasper didn't realise was that, deep in his pocket, the two rats had woken up and were listening with great interest to every word that was said.

11

Two Surprises for Rags and Bags

That very night, Rags and Bags set out to look for the Green Marvel in the kitchen, but things didn't go at all according to plan. To begin with, they got into the dumb-waiter again, but when it descended and the doors opened they found to their surprise that they were in the drawing room instead of the kitchen.

They hopped out and looked around. It wasn't where they wanted to be, but everything in the house was still new to them and therefore fascinating. There was an armchair beside the fire, and on the table beside it was a book and some knitting, with the needles stuck into the ball of wool. 'This must be where Mrs Haverford-Snuffley sits in the evening,' Bags said.

They climbed up on to the table to have a better look at everything, and saw that there was a third thing there they hadn't been able to see from the floor. It was a cardboard box with a pink ribbon on the lid and some gold writing that the rats, being rats, couldn't read. But they pushed the lid off anyway to have a peek at what was inside.

The box was full of small brown objects. Although they were all more or less the same size, they were a range of different shapes. Some were square and some heart-shaped. Some looked like leaves and some like little barrels. One was a smooth dome and another was a ridged whorl. And all of them had the most marvellous, delicious mouth-watering smell. What could they possibly be?

I would like to ask you now to do something

difficult. I'd like you to imagine that you're a rat. You've never in all your life heard the word 'chocolate'. Even if you saw it written down, it wouldn't mean anything to you because, being a rat, you can't read. 'Chocolate' could mean anything. It could mean 'tadpole' or 'sausage' or 'handbag'.

Nor have you ever come across chocolate the thing, rather than chocolate the word before. You don't know anything about it. You don't even know that you can eat it. You don't know that it can come as a bar that can be broken into squares. You don't know that it can be a yummy hot drink. And above all you don't know that it can be made into actual chocolates: small, bite-sized pieces, each with a different filling – toffee or strawberry cream or hazelnut or orange, each one more delicious than the one before.

So imagine what it's like to be a rat and to stumble across your first ever box of chocolates, there for the taking!

'I don't know what these are, Bags, but they smell great. I'll give one a lick just to try it out.'

Cautiously Rags licked one of the little brown things . . . and a look of total bliss crossed his snout. 'Oh, Bags!' he said. 'OH, BAGS!' and he scoffed the chocolate down in one gulp.

It was a total free-for-all after that. Lemon Surprises and Caramel Hearts, Turkish Delights and Coconut Clusters: the rats set to and gobbled them all up until they were so full they could hardly stand, and the box with the pink ribbon was empty.

'Never could I have imagined that something could be so scrumptious!' Bags sighed as he polished off the last Marzipan Dream.

'Even if we never again get to eat whatever these things are, I will remember this night for the rest of my life, yes, until I am an old grey rat with faded fur and trembling paws,' Rags declared.

But they were to remember the night for

another reason too, and it wouldn't be such a pleasant memory.

When they crept out of the drawing room, they found that they were once more in the hallway of the big house, where a small lamp burned as before.

'I don't really feel like looking for the Green Marvel now,' Bags said.

'Neither do I. Not after all the excitement we've already had. I think we should go back to bed now and start looking for the necklace tomorrow night.' Bags agreed with Rags.

'Now, which way is Jasper's bedroom?'

And that was when IT happened. Suddenly they felt a tremendous cold wind, coming from something flapping above their heads. The light of the small lamp was blotted out and an icy darkness enveloped them. Just with that, something grabbed them both by the scruff of their necks and whipped them clean off their paws, up into the air. What on earth was happening?

They had been grabbed by an enormous bat! Its immense black wings had caused darkness to fall as it swooped down to snatch them, and now it flew madly around the hallway in jagged and juddering flight, with its two captives dangling beneath it. As you may imagine, rats don't scare easily, but Bags and Rags were terrified. It was like being on some horrible fairground ride, where you're swung around a thousand times in different ways and your tummy turns over and there's nothing you can do to stop all of this happening. Rags came within a whisker of having his head banged on the frame of the hall mirror, and Bags was sure, quite sure, that they were going to crash straight into the crystal chandelier that hung high up on the ceiling. Instead of that, the big bat flew round and round the chandelier, until the two rats were so dizzy they thought they were going to faint, or be sick, or both. And at that point, the bat let them go.

65

Down, down, down they fell and landed *crump* on a thick soft rug. Gazing up in terror, they could see that the big bat had come to roost on the chandelier. It was a most peculiar sight, for it was hanging upside down from a crystal branch, and it was wearing a knitted woollen hat, pulled tightly on to its head.

'You leave Nelly be!' it cried. 'If you bully her again, you'll have me to answer to. Do you understand?'

The two rats nodded.

'DO YOU UNDERSTAND?' the bat roared.

'Yes! Yes!' they squeaked.

'We're really sorry we were mean to her,' Bags whimpered. 'We won't steal her hat ever again.'

'If you do, you're in big trouble,' the bat said. 'What happened tonight is nothing compared to what I'll do to you if you annoy Nelly one more time.'

'We'll be good! We'll be good!' the two rats

cried. 'We promise to behave.'

And this time when they said it, they didn't have their claws crossed.

12

Jasper Gets a Scolding

Jasper was quite looking forward to the following day because he had the afternoon off.

'Wakey-wakey lads,' he cried, opening the drawer where the rats slept. 'Get up and have your breakfast.' He offered them small pieces of fruit and little crusts from his own meal, but to his amazement, Rags and Bags weren't interested. This isn't like them at all, he thought, as they turned their snouts up at the food and rolled over in their sock sleeping-bags. Never before had he known them to refuse anything edible, for they were the greediest creatures imaginable. They must be feeling really poorly. He decided to leave the food for them on a saucer and to let them sleep while he went off to work in the garden.

He was half-heartedly weeding a flower bed about an hour later when he noticed Mrs Haverford-Snuffley approach. Oddly enough, she wasn't smiling and waving as usual but looked quite serious and even a little bit cross.

'Dear lady, why this cloud upon your lovely features? What is it that troubles you?' Jasper asked, smarmy as ever.

'This is most embarrassing, Professor Orchid. I don't want to have to ask you this but I feel that I must. The thing is – oh dear me, there's no easy way to put this question so I have to say it bluntly. Did you eat my chocolates?'

Jasper had been grinning at her as she spoke, but at this, the grin vanished from his face. 'Your chocolates? Why, of course I didn't! How could you possibly think such a thing?'

'Because I had a whole boxful of them

yesterday and now they're all gone. I left them in the drawing room, beside my knitting, when I went to bed last night and now they're gone, every last one of them.'

Jasper stared at her, baffled. 'Could it have been the bat?' he asked, pointing at the little creature dangling from the feather and thinking that even if it wasn't, here perhaps was a chance to get it into trouble. 'Let's face it, it is quite spoiled, isn't it?'

'Mummy's little treasure doesn't eat chocolate, does she?' Mrs Haverford-Snuffley said, looking sideways at Nelly, who bounced up and down vigorously at this. 'It's too heavy and rich for her tummy-wummy.'

'What about that Knuttmegg woman then? I wouldn't put it past her to have scoffed the lot.'

'No, it can't be her either. Even though she's a cook, you'd be surprised how few sweets and goodies Mrs Knuttmegg eats. That's why she's so skinny. She eats a tiny Easter egg once a year and a little chocolate Santa at Christmas, and that's it. And in any case, I just know she would never do a thing like that.' Mrs Haverford-Snuffley bit her lower lip and frowned. 'It was Mrs Knuttmegg who suggested that I ask you about it. I told her just a short while ago, and she said to me that she'd had food disappearing from the kitchen recently too. "Ever since that gardener fellow arrived," she said, "food's been vanishing in this house as if there were rats."'

And as soon as he heard this, Jasper knew exactly what had happened to the chocolates.

'Dear madam,' he exclaimed in dismay, 'do please forgive me!'

Mrs Haverford-Snuffley stared at him in amazement. 'So you did eat them.'

'No. I mean yes. I mean No! No! No! No! No!'

Mrs Haverford-Snuffley took this as a 'Yes'.

'Well I must say, Professor Orchid,' she remarked coldly, 'I'm astonished at this. I'd never have thought it of a gentleman like you.

I didn't even want to ask but Mrs Knuttmegg insisted it could be no one else. Please don't let it happen again.' She waved aside Jasper's grovelling attempts at an explanation and trotted off across the garden again, with her bat companion.

As soon as lunchtime came and his work was over for the day, Jasper raced up to his room. He now realised that the rats hadn't been sick at all. They'd just been stuffed with chocolates when last he saw them and that was why they hadn't wanted their breakfast. Now they were bouncing around the place, delighted with themselves. While he'd been out working they had got their appetites back, and the saucer of food had been licked clean.

'Oh, why won't you be good!' he shouted. 'If you get me into trouble again I'll get the sack. Then I'll have to leave Haverford-Snuffley Hall immediately and I'll never find the Green Marvel. Why won't you behave yourselves?'

The rats just laughed at him.

Jasper had planned to spend his afternoon off looking for the necklace, but instead he went into Woodford. He didn't manage to get a lift this time so he had to wait ages for the bus. When he got there he bought a huge box of Woodford Creams. These were the expensive and delicious rose-scented chocolates for which the town was famous and of which Jasper himself had eaten vast quantities in his old life. To buy the Creams took an enormous whack out of the money the prison officer had given him. He had wanted to keep that money for himself, but he felt he had to get back in Mrs Haverford-Snuffley's good books as soon as possible.

As the woman in the shop was wrapping up the box she kept looking at Jasper. 'Do I know you?' she said at last. 'I think your face is familiar to me.'

'I've never been here in my life before,' Jasper lied. 'You must be mixing me up with someone else.' He paid for the chocolates and as she was giving him his change she said all of a sudden, 'I know who it is you remind me of! If it wasn't for that big black beard, you'd look exactly like Jas—'

But before she could finish what she was saying, Jasper was already out of the shop and halfway down the street, as fast as he could run.

 **13**

Strange Music

The following morning, when Jasper was on his way out to work, Mrs Knuttmegg came out of the kitchen and handed him a bucket with a lid on it.

'What's this all about?'

'It's for the compost heap,' she said. 'You know where the orchard is, with the high wall all around it? At the back of that, beside the potting shed, you'll find the compost heap.' Without another word she went back into the kitchen and slammed the door closed.

As soon as he was outside, Jasper lifted the lid of the bucket and peeped in. 'Oh yuk!'

To his disgust, it was full to the brim with potato peelings and egg shells, old tea bags and turnip tops. 'How dare she! The cheek of it! Who does that woman think she is, handing a pile of muck like that to me? ME, Jasper Jellit!'

He wanted to go back inside and empty the whole lot over Mrs Knutmegg's head, right there in the middle of her own kitchen, but he knew that he had to behave himself, especially after all that business with the chocolates.

Thinking of this, he patted his pockets to make sure that the rats were there. Yes, he could feel them through the cloth of his jacket. He was going to have to keep a strict eye on them from now on, to make sure that they didn't get him into any more trouble.

He was in for an even bigger shock when he got to the back of the orchard. Right beside the shed was an enormous heap of kitchen waste, spilling out of the top of a big wooden crate. Jasper knew nothing at all about gardens, and so he didn't know that if you pile up lots of old vegetable peelings and coffee grounds, banana skins and so on, they will rot, and all the worms will get to work on them. In no time at all you'll have a lovely rich brown compost to put on your flowers and plants, to make them grow strong and healthy.

Jasper thought that Mrs Knutmegg was nasty and crazy and that she did strange things like this just to spite him.

It has to be said that the compost heap smelt pretty horrible. Holding his nose, Jasper took the lid off the bucket and poured the contents on to the pile of rotting mush. 'Yuk and double yuk!' he cried. 'Yuk three times!'

All at once, Rags and Bags hopped out of his pocket. Rats aren't too fussy about what they eat, and, smelling all the decaying food, they thought that there might be a few tasty-bites going. But just before they could dive in, something very strange happened.

Music began to play. It seemed to be coming from the orchard, on the other side of the wall, where someone was playing a flute. Oh but it was the saddest music you can imagine! It was mournful and slow, a heartbreaking melody. Jasper had been cross up until then, but now he felt very gloomy. The rats had been just about to dive into the pile of kitchen scraps, but they stopped dead. They stood there with their ears flat on their heads, and their whiskers drooping.

'Isn't this miserable, lads?' Jasper said, and he began to sob. The two rats nodded. They threw their little paws around each other and they also began to cry, tears pouring down their snouts as they hugged each other and wept. 'Boo hoo hoo!' Jasper wailed. 'I want my mammy!' Never in all his life had he felt so unhappy. He pulled out his hanky and blew his nose. On and on the music went. The rats were lying on the ground now, sobbing their beady eyes out.

Just when they all thought they couldn't bear it for another minute, the music began to fade away. As it did, the mood began to change.

Jasper didn't feel quite so bad now. He put away his hanky. The rats sat up and sniffed and gulped. They wiped the last of their tears away with their paws. The music faded and grew fainter, until there was silence but for the sound of the breeze in the branches of the trees. They all felt foolish and strange and wondered what had come over them.

'This is the oddest, most unpleasant place I've ever been,' Jasper muttered to himself. 'If only I could find the Green Marvel. Then I could leave, never to return!'

14

Nelly Has an Idea

Going down in the dumb-waiter that night Rags and Bags both felt extremely nervous and hoped they wouldn't meet the big bat again. They wanted to go to the kitchen but still didn't know how to work the dumb-waiter properly, and much to their annoyance when the doors opened they discovered that they were in the drawing room again. This time there was nothing to eat, as Mrs Haverford-Snuffley had had the good sense to hide her chocolates before she went to bed. There was no getting away from it: as they continued their exploration of the house they were going to have to go through the hallway, whether they liked it or not.

To their great relief, there was no sign of the big bat, but Nelly was there as usual, hanging upside down from the edge of the table, with her pale bonnet firmly tied on to her head.

'Hello, Nelly! How are you?'

'I'm all right,' she replied cautiously.

'Love the hat! It really suits you.' She didn't reply to this, but scowled down at them.

'We're really sorry we were mean to you,' Rags said, 'and we promise we won't ever do anything like that ever again.'

Nelly narrowed her eyes. 'Did Benny have a word with you?'

'Benny? Who's he?'

'My big brother.'

The two rats nodded. 'He, er, he sort of pointed out to us that we hadn't been very kind to you,' Rags said.

'But we knew that anyway,' Bags added.

'And we will be nice from now on. Incredibly nice.'

And then Nelly said something that astonished them.

'Can I be your friend?'

'You?' Bags replied before he could stop himself. 'But you're a girl! A soppy girl, and a bat into the bargain! We couldn't poss— Ouch!' Rags had given him a sudden sharp kick in the shins.

'Of course you can be our friend!' he cried. 'There's nothing we would like better. We were just about to ask you the same thing. I'm Rags and this is Bags. We'll make a great team, the three of us.'

'Oh, goody,' said Nelly. 'I'm so pleased. Now tell me, what are you up to? What are you doing prowling around the house in the middle of the night?'

'We're looking for the Green Marvel,' Rags said. 'Have you ever heard of it? Do you know what it is?'

'I do, of course,' Nelly replied. 'It's a necklace. Look, you can see it here in the painting.' She unfurled her wings from her sides and fluttered up to settle on the golden frame. The rats were hugely impressed that she could do this. Even if she was a soppy girl, it was quite something to be able to fly.

'Where are you looking?' she asked.

'That's the problem,' Rags said. 'We hardly know where to begin. Do you have any ideas?'

'Well, we could ask, I suppose.'

'Ask who?'

'Why Georgiana, of course. The woman in the painting. It was her necklace, after all, so she might be able to help.'

Rags and Bags looked at each other. What a strange little creature this bat was! What could she possibly mean? 'Georgiana's my friend,' Nelly prattled on. 'She likes me lots. I haven't seen her in a while but we could go and ask her right now. Will we do that?'

'Why not?' Rags said, thinking it was best

to humour her. 'We have no other plans for the night.'

'Very good then,' Nelly cried. 'I'll take you to her room. Follow me!'

15

Georgiana

The little bat fluttered up the wide staircase and the rats scampered after her. She then led them down a long narrow corridor until they came to a door at the end of it, which stood half open.

'In here,' she whispered.

There was a lovely moon that night. A cool silvery light shone through the high windows so that Rags and Bags could see where they were. The room was prettily furnished, like a little parlour, with a sofa and two chairs covered in yellow silk. The curtains were tied back with thick tasselled cords. There was a bookcase full of small books, bound in leather, and a marble mantelpiece on which sat a golden clock.

'But there's nobody here,' Bags said.

'I have to call her,' Nelly replied. 'I'll do it now but you won't be able to hear me.'

'What do you mean?'

'I have a special high-pitched call. People like Georgiana can hear it and other bats, but nobody else. Mrs Haverford-Snuffley can't hear it either and she doesn't even know about it.'

Nelly opened her mouth wide. It was red and moist against her dark furry body and it was full of narrow, pointed teeth. Rags and Bags thought she looked incredibly creepy. She gave a second silent cry.

And then it happened.

A beautiful young woman came into the room. The rats recognised her immediately from the painting downstairs. She had the same white skin and straight nose. Her reddish curls were piled high on top of her head and she was wearing a dark blue silk dress. But she didn't come through the door. She came straight through the wall. And with that Rags and Bags realised that she was a . . .

'GHOST! AAARRRRGH! IT'S A GHOST! HELP! AAARGGHHH! GHOST! GHOST!'

And in exactly the same moment that they saw Georgiana, she saw them. She pulled her long dress up around her shins and jumped on to a chair.

'RATS! AAAAARRGH! HELP! HELP! RATS! AAAAARRRRGH!'

Rags and Bags ran to the far side of the room and clung to each other in terror. Georgiana's face had gone bright red from all the screaming. But when all three of them stopped to draw breath, they could hear the sound of Nelly laughing.

'I never heard such a fuss in my life,' she cried. 'There's nothing for anybody to be frightened about. Georgiana, get down from that chair and let me introduce you. Rags and Bags, come out of that corner into the middle of the room.'

Very cautiously they did as Nelly commanded. 'These are my new best friends,' the bat said. 'They wanted to meet you.'

'But they're rats,' Georgiana insisted.

'And you're a ghost,' Bags said. Georgiana shrugged her shoulders, so much as to say, Well, there's nothing I can do about that, is there? But she was a polite, well-brought-up girl so she said, 'How d'you do?' and she gave them a nod of the head. 'You'll excuse me if I don't shake your . . . paws.'

'Not at all! Not at all!' The rats had no wish to be touched by a ghost. They were very much regretting that they had agreed to meet her. They knew about ghosts because when they were living in the jail, there had been one particular prisoner who used to tell ghost stories to the other inmates, to pass the time on the long dark winter evenings. The rats had used to hide under the chairs and listen in. They'd enjoyed every minute of it; they'd loved the thrill of a good fright.

But Georgiana wasn't quite what they'd have expected in a ghost. For one thing, she wasn't transparent. In spite of being able to walk through walls, she looked as solid as Jasper did. The rats also made the mistake of thinking she was pretty because she was a ghost. Having been born and brought up in a men's prison, Rags and Bags had actually seen very few women. Of those that they did know, including Mrs Haverford-Snuffley, Mrs Knuttmegg and the café woman in the greasy pinny, none of them were great beauties. Georgiana, on the other hand, was loveliness itself. Her beauty was enhanced by a pearly light that surrounded her and that further gently illuminated the room. The rats guessed that this must have something to do with being a ghost, and although they found it spooky, they also thought there was something quite attractive about it.

'I'll sit here,' Georgiana said, settling herself on the sofa in her billowing silk dress, 'and why don't you, Nelly my love, hang off the back of that chair over there, where I can see you? As for you pair,' she said to the rats, 'you can go there.' She pointed out to Rags and Bags a velvet footstool near to where she was sitting. 'Not too close, mind.' She pushed the stool away a bit with her toe, which pleased them, because they had no more desire to sit right beside her than she had to sit beside them.

'Rags and Bags are looking for the Green Marvel,' Nelly said.

'Oh, if only I knew where it was!' she cried. 'I still can't believe I was so foolish. My necklace! My wonderful emerald necklace!'

'I never thought to ask you this before, but where did you get it from?'

'It was a present, Nelly dear,' Georgiana said. 'There was a very rich man who wanted to marry me and he gave it to me. He said that it matched my eyes. And it did, you know. Look here!'

Quite suddenly and unexpectedly she bent down to where the rats were sitting, and opened her eyes wide. They were indeed green – but of such a green! Green as a fresh bright leaf, green as the ocean in a hidden cove, green, yes, green as emeralds beyond price.

'He told me that if I'd had blue eyes, he'd have given me sapphires.'

'And I suppose if you'd had red eyes, he'd have offered you rubies,' Rags suggested. Georgiana stared at him coldly for some moments and then said, 'I'm not too sure if I like your new friends, Nelly.'

'And did you marry him, Georgiana?' the little bat asked quickly. 'Did you marry the man who gave you the Green Marvel?'

'Of course not! He was an absolute nitwit. He was silly and proud. He thought that just because he had pots of money and gave me emeralds I was certain to marry him. I doubt very much if he tried the same trick with another girl. I think I taught him a good lesson when I took the necklace.'

'But then you lost it,' Bags said.

'I did,' she admitted. 'I lost it. I don't know where it is.'

'Can't you remember where you had it last?' Rags asked.

'Well, I do know that the last time I saw it was about two hundred years ago, Mister Smarty-Pants Rat, so I can hardly be blamed if I've forgotten, now can I? What I do know is that I hid it somewhere to keep it safe and I wrote this little note to remind me where it was, only now I can't understand it.'

From a small gold purse hanging at her side she took a slip of paper and unfolded it. 'I'll read it aloud to you.'

'"Folly 'twould be
To lose a jewel like me".'

She paused, and the three small animals waited for her to continue.

'Well, go on then,' Bags urged after a moment.
'That's it.'

'That's it? Nothing else?'

Embarrassed, Georgiana shook her curls to say 'No' as the two rats stared at her in dismay.

But Nelly was delighted. 'It's a kind of riddle,' she cried. 'Oh, I love things like this! Every morning Mrs Haverford-Snuffley does the crossword in the *Woodford Trumpet* and I do it too. I work out all the clues. I'm much quicker at it than Mrs Haverford-Snuffley, even though I'm reading it upside down,' she added proudly. 'Read it again, Georgiana.' The ghost smoothed out the paper on her lap.

'"Folly 'twould be

'To lose a jewel like me." "Folly" means "stupidity". So it's saying "It would be stupid to lose a jewel like me."'

'Well, that's really helpful, I must say,' Bags remarked sarcastically.

'But "folly" could also mean "a folly" – you know, the thing in the garden!'

'Why, of course! Why did I not think of that? Gosh, Nelly, you're so bright,' Georgiana said admiringly. But now the rats were baffled.

'Er, what thing in the garden? What do you mean? What's a folly?'

'In my day,' the ghost said, 'there was a fashion for putting little buildings in gardens for no real reason, just because they looked nice. Stone pillars, ruins, that kind of thing.'

'Ruins? Isn't a ruin what you get when a building falls down?'

'Yes, but these were built as ruins in the first place.'

The more she tried to explain, the more she baffled the rats. 'Why on earth would anyone build a ruin?'

'I don't know. I can only tell you that it seemed like a good idea at the time.'

'Our folly is exceptionally nice,' Nelly said. 'It's not a ruin, it's a small circular building like a temple, with stone seats in it.'

'And is that where the Green Marvel is hidden?'

Georgiana glanced down again at the note in her hand and then looked up at the animals, suddenly excited.

'It sounds as if it must be!'

16

Jasper in the Garden

The following morning, to Jasper's great surprise, the rats were absolutely determined that they would go out into the garden with him. He would have much preferred that they stayed locked up in the room, because they had a habit of getting into mischief when they were out and about. But just as he was leaving the room they raced across the floor. They ran up his legs, like two squirrels climbing a tree, and hopped into his inside pocket. He plucked them out by the scruffs of their necks and dropped them back in their drawer, but they scampered out again and clung to his ankles as he walked back to the door. With this, he gave up.

'All right then,' he said, 'you can come out to the garden. But always remember – you have to behave! You have to be good!' The two rats grinned as he removed them from his legs and lifted them into his pockets.

When he clumped down the wooden stairs he found Mrs Knuttmegg waiting there, just outside the kitchen door. To his surprise, she didn't sneer at him or make the usual sarcastic remarks; in fact she looked surprisingly ill at ease. Seeing her there reminded him of something.

'That horrible screaming in the middle of the night,' Jasper said, 'what was that all about? Was that you? It woke me out of a sound sleep.' Instead of making some smart remark as he expected, Mrs Knuttmegg just stared at him with wide round eyes. She was clearly very frightened.

'So you heard it too,' she whispered. 'Tell me, what exactly did it say? I thought it was

"Cats! Cats" and lots of screaming, but Missus thought it was "Bats! Bats!"'

'Well, she would say that, wouldn't she?' Jasper replied. 'I don't know. I couldn't make out any words. But what do you mean, "it"? Who was that screaming, if it wasn't you or Mrs Haverford-Snuffley?'

'It was the ghost,' Mrs Knuttmegg said. 'Didn't you know that there's a ghost in this house?'

'Don't be so silly! There's no such a thing as a ghost,' Jasper said.

'Well, if there isn't, who was that screaming last night? It wasn't me and it wasn't the missus.'

'It certainly wasn't me either, although it seems to be quite the thing to blame me for everything that goes wrong around here,' Jasper snapped, as he flounced out to the garden to begin his day's work.

He spent the morning weeding flower beds. There was no gardening work he really liked but he particularly hated weeding. It was hard labour, and because he didn't know anything at all it was easy to get it wrong, and rip up the flowers instead of the weeds. He started on a long, curved flower bed and by mid-morning he had worked his way round to the front of the house, where he discovered Mrs Haverford-Snuffley asleep in the sun in a deckchair. A crumpled copy of the *Woodford Trumpet* lay on the ground beside her, where it had fallen from her hands. Being very careful not to wake her up, Jasper tiptoed over until he was standing right beside her.

The small bat hanging from the feather was asleep too. Ugh, how Jasper hated it! It made him mad to think of a nasty, ugly little creature like that being so pampered and spoiled. He wished he could play a trick on it. Maybe if he was very careful he could reach in and open the ribbons of its bonnet. Then its hat would fall off and it might get into trouble for being careless. But when he looked at it closely the ribbon was tightly knotted and Jasper knew that his fingers would never be nimble enough to undo it without his being noticed.

And then he had another, even meaner idea. He pressed his middle finger firmly behind his thumb, turning his right hand into a kind of catapult. He would flick the bat off the end of the feather and into the middle of next week! Or at least into the middle of the lawn, he thought, sniggering to himself and carefully taking aim.

But at that very moment, he got a sudden and terrible shock. One of the rats – he would never know which one – bit him on his tummy with its pointed teeth, and a sharp, painful nip it was.

'Oh that's agony. AGONY!'

It happened just as he was about to attack Nelly and it made him stumble and lose his footing. Instead of flicking away the bat, he flicked Mrs Haverford–Snuffley hard on the nose just as he tumbled and fell on top of her. The deckchair collapsed and they both ended up in a tangled heap on the ground, all mixed up with the sheets of the newspaper.

'Professor Orchid, this is outrageous! What on earth is happening? My nose, my poor nose.'

'The bat did it!' Jasper screamed. 'It's all the bat's fault!'

'I'm sure Mummy's little darling wasn't to blame at all.'

And in the mad confusion that followed, Jasper didn't notice that the rats had slipped quietly out of his pocket and scampered off.

How Do We Get There?

They ran and ran as fast as they could, off down the gravel path and round the side of the house, where they stopped for a moment.

'Do you think he saw us?' Rags said, gasping for breath.

'No, but he'll soon notice that we're gone. Let's get to that folly thing.'

Nelly and Georgiana had given them directions: at the back of the house turn right, away from the kitchen garden. Go straight along until you come to the greenhouse, and then turn left. Go straight on, turn left again at the big oak and after a short while they would see the folly before them. They were good clear directions, and before long the two rats saw in the distance a small building of grey stone. It was circular, with pillars all around it and a domed roof. It was exactly as it had been described to them.

'That's it! That's the folly!' Bags said excitedly. But as they got closer they realised to their dismay that Nelly and Georgiana had left out one significant detail.

The folly stood on an island in the middle of a small lake.

'Oh no! Now what are we to do?' They stared across the water in silence for a few moments and then Rags said stoutly, 'Well, I'm not giving up. We're just going to have to find a way of getting there.'

They talked for quite some time about making a little boat or a raft. They looked around and found a few pieces of wood, but they were all too small.

'There's nothing else for it. We're going to

have to swim.'

'Do we know how to?' Rags asked. 'I don't know if I can. I've never tried.'

'Swim? Of course we can swim. We're rats, after all. Have you forgotten about Great-Great-Great-Uncle Dinny?'

Although Rags and Bags were prison rats, as were their mum and dad and grannies and grandads, there had been lots of stories in the family about other rats, cousins and aunties and great-uncles, who had led quite different lives. There was cousin Joey, whose home had been in a flour mill, and who had lived the kind of life the prison rats could only dream about. All the grain he could eat! Great shiny golden heaps of wheat! He would eat his bellyful as often as he wanted, and then sleep it off in the sun beside the mill-race, as the water tumbled over the mill-wheel.

But more legendary still had been Great-Great-Great-Uncle Dinny, who had lived many years ago on a trade-ship. He wore a small gold ear-ring, they had been told, and he had tattoos on both forepaws, one of an anchor and one of a heart with the word MUM in it. He ate oranges and spices every day, and at night he slept curled up in bales of coloured silk.

Then the day came when his ship was attacked by pirates. A cannon ball blew a hole in the side of the ship and the sea poured in. So what did Great-Great-Great-Uncle Dinny do? He immediately became the Rat Who Deserted the Sinking Ship. Amidst all the shouting of the crew, the smoke and the gushing of the water, he hopped over the side without so much as a backward glance, and started swimming. He swam and he swam for days, until he came to a tropical island. 'I was getting tired of life at sea anyway,' he said to himself, as he plodded up the hot white sand. There were coconut groves on the island, and banana trees and pineapples, and Dinny had lived there happily ever after. Rags and Bags' mum had told them this story so many times when they were small rats. They thought of it now as they stared at the grey water of the lake.

'He swam for days,' Bags said. 'Days and days.'

'Maybe it wasn't true.'

'Rags! How can you even think such a thing!'

Rags shrugged. 'It looks cold,' he said, pointing at the lake, 'but I suppose there's nothing else for it.'

They stepped into the water together, pulling faces and going 'Oh! Oh! Oh!' because the water was indeed very cold; but, fair play to them, they kept going. As they moved out of their depth, they kicked and flicked their legs, not quite sure what they should be doing, and hoping it would work out.

And it did.

'Look! Look at me!' Bags cried. 'I'm swimming!'

'Me too!'

They weren't very good at it, but they weren't bad either, given that it was their first attempt. Bags found it hard to swim in a straight line, and kept drifting off course. Rags, try as he might, couldn't help splashing water up his own snout, which was most unpleasant. To begin with, they were just pleased to be able to do it, but as time passed the novelty wore off. It seemed to take forever, and they were both shivering with cold and exhausted by the time they finally reached the island and stumbled up the steps of the folly.

18

The Folly

To their relief, the folly didn't have a proper door, just an open archway through which they went. In the shelter of the building they shook the water of the lake from their pelts, and looked around them, starting to get quite excited again. 'Just think, at any moment now, we could find the Green Marvel!'

The folly was circular, with six high rectangular windows. Against the walls were two curved benches made of stone, and the floor was covered in big square grey flagstones. They looked under the benches, but there was nothing there. Where could the emerald necklace be hidden? Puzzled, the two rats scratched their heads. The problem was that there was nowhere else to look. Apart from the benches, the folly was completely empty. There were no cupboards or boxes, no little nooks where something might be concealed.

'This is a stupid place anyway,' Bags grumbled. 'I don't see the point of it.'

'Maybe the bat got it wrong,' Rags said, as he walked across the floor. But as he did so, he noticed something. *One of the stones moved beneath his paws!* He stopped and thought about this, then carefully inspected the flagstone. It was identical to all the others except for one small detail: it had a crack running across it, which marked off a triangle in one corner. And that little corner, Rags now saw as he bounced up and down on it, was quite loose.

'There could be something hidden under it. Help me, Bags, quickly!'

It didn't take them long to prise up the broken piece of stone, and Bags held it while

Rags looked underneath.

'Hurry up! This thing's heavy.'

'There's nothing there,' Rags said, with terrible disappointment in his voice.

'Nothing at all?'

'No necklace. No jewels. Just a measly piece of paper, exactly like the one Georgiana had, the one with the clue written on it.'

'Urrrrgh . . . well, grab it, you nitwit,' Bags cried. 'And hurry up, I can't hold this thing forever.' Rags darted his paw in and had just managed to snatch out the note before Bags's strength gave out, as he let the triangle of stone fall back into place, just missing Rags's head.

'Really, I wonder about you sometimes,' Bags said crossly. '"Nothing there"! Give that note to me. I'll keep it safe and give it to Georgiana.' Not for the first time in their lives the rats regretted that they didn't know how to read.

'Sorry,' Rags said meekly. 'I suppose we should think of heading back.'

'I suppose so.' Neither of them was looking forward to getting into the cold water of the lake again.

'Look, there's another doorway.' Rags pointed to the far side of the folly. 'Let's have a peek through there. Perhaps we won't have to swim quite so far this time.'

But when they went over to the doorway and looked out, they couldn't believe their eyes. It wasn't just that the distance between the folly and the land was much shorter on this side – it was that there was an elegant little humpbacked bridge across the narrow channel of water.

'Yippee! We don't have to swim at all!'

Rags and Bags scampered across the bridge and then went around the edge of the lake. In the distance they could see Haverford-Snuffley Hall. It would be a bit of a walk home but that didn't bother them because they weren't in a hurry. They took it in turns to carry the note they had found.

'What do you say we go home via the kitchen garden?' Bags suggested. 'Stop off for a little something.'

'I couldn't agree more,' Rags replied.

There was a high ivy-covered wall around the kitchen garden, and as the rats drew near, they saw someone they didn't recognise. It was a young man with fair hair cut in a wide blunt fringe. He was dressed in soft brown work-clothes. 'Another gardener, by the look of it,' Bags whispered. 'Jasper will be delighted. He'll make him do all the work.'

But as he spoke, something extraordinary happened. The young man walked up to the wall and then *he walked straight through it!*

'How did he do that? Where's he gone?' The rats ran up and slipped through the gate into the kitchen garden to see where he was, but there was no sign of the young man anywhere.

They might have thought more about this had they not been immediately distracted by all the scrumptious fruit and vegetables that were there for the taking. The warm, sun-ripened tomatoes were a big hit, and then they feasted on soft fruit.

'Do you know what I think, Bags?' Rags said as he popped a sweet pink hairy gooseberry in his mouth.

'What?'

'We should get out more!'

And the two rats fell about laughing.

Jasper Starts Searching

Meanwhile, back at the house, Jasper had managed to talk his way out of trouble yet again. After making all kinds of excuses to Mrs Haverford-Snuffley about why he had flicked her on the nose and knocked her off her chair, he suddenly cried, 'Ooh, I feel dizzy! The whole garden's going round and round. That must be what happened earlier, that's why I fell over. Oooh, everything's spinning!'

'If you feel unwell, Professor Orchid, then you can't be blamed for what happened. You should look after yourself. Perhaps you've been working too hard. I think you should go back to bed. Take the rest of today off work.'

'Madam, you are kind; you are too kind,' he said. But in his heart he was thinking, *Missus, you are such a dozy old bat even a toddler would be smarter than you.* 'Thank you! Thank you!' he cried. 'Oh, it's starting again. There goes the greenhouse, flying past my head. Goodness me, I'm so dizzy, it's horrible.'

'You poor man. Off you go to your bed and I'll get Mrs Knuttmegg to send you up something nice to eat.'

Fat chance of that, Jasper thought, as he went into the house and up the stairs, holding on to the walls and pretending to stagger. And sure enough, as he was putting on his pyjamas to go back to bed, he could hear shouting the whole way from the kitchen. 'DIZZY? TREATS? I'LL GIVE HIM TREATS!'

I bet you will, Jasper thought, as he pulled back the covers and got into bed. When the dumb-waiter comes up, I'm not even going to bother to open it. Who knows what horrors she'll have put into it. A plate of cold cabbage, perhaps. Yuk! Or a pile of tongue sandwiches. Double yuk! Still, he thought as he snuggled down under the blankets, it was great not to have to work.

He slept soundly for a few hours, and had sweet dreams: sweet to Jasper, that is, for to anyone else they would have seemed strange and unpleasant. He dreamt about being nasty and mean, of bossing people about and of everyone being afraid of him.

He awoke feeling relaxed and refreshed, he was cheerful and full of plans. But as he finished getting dressed again, he happened to glance out of the window. 'Oh no!' There were Rags and Bags, on their way home from the folly, stuffing themselves with soft fruit in the kitchen garden.

'Those wretched creatures! Why can't they behave themselves? Why won't they be good?' he moaned, which, I'm sure you will agree, was a bit much coming from the likes of Jasper.

As soon as he was ready, he crept downstairs, hoping not to be seen. He had decided that he was going to search for the Green Marvel, and he was going to begin in the library. This might seem like an odd place to start, but Jasper had his reasons. When he had had his own big house, he had also had a library – not that he cared anything for books or reading. In fact, books meant so little to him that he used to cut out the bits with all the words, leaving just the surrounding frame of paper, so that it still looked like a book when it was shut, but actually had a big hole in the middle where he could hide things. The thought occurred to him that perhaps someone in Haverford-Snuffley Hall had had the same idea, and that that was where the Green Marvel was hidden. (And I can tell you now that it wasn't.)

In any case, Jasper spent the rest of the afternoon down in the library, simply taking books off the shelves, opening them and then putting them back. It took a long time because there were hundreds of them. He was so absorbed in what he was doing that he didn't notice when the library door quietly opened, and Mrs Knuttmegg stood there, looking in. To begin with, her eyes grew round with amazement as she watched Jasper engaged in his strange task, but gradually they changed again, and grew narrow with suspicion. Still Jasper leafed through the books and still she watched him, and when at last she did slip away again, he didn't see her leave.

20

Georgiana Is Upset

'You might have mentioned the bridge.'

'The bridge!' Nelly said. 'Gosh, I completely forgot to tell you about that.' It was night-time, and they had all gathered together again in Georgiana's room. 'If we'd known about the bridge, we wouldn't have had to swim there,' Bags said.

'It was cold,' Rags added. 'It was horrible. We almost drowned.'

'You poor things,' Georgiana said soothingly. 'You were both so brave.' She was sitting on the sofa in her flouncy dress, surrounded in the same soft, pearly glow of light that they had noticed on the first evening. She leaned down and stared at them with her wondrous green eyes, and then she patted them both quickly on the heads. 'Good boys!'

Rags and Bags were thrilled by this unexpected kindness. No one was *ever* nice to them. People used to scream and run away when they saw them, or even threw things at them, so they were dazzled by this attention.

'Did you like the folly?' Georgiana asked. 'Isn't it the most wonderful place?'

'I couldn't quite see the point of it myself,' Rags admitted, and Bags nodded his head in agreement.

'I used to think it was a very good place to meet people,' Georgiana said. 'It's quiet and far away from the house, so if you wanted to sneak off, and see somebody you weren't supposed to be with, you could do it and no one would ever know.' There was a strange expression on her face as she said this, wistful and a little bit sad, and the rats thought it made her look even lovelier than she usually did.

'Never mind all that,' said Nelly, who was beginning to get impatient. 'What about the Green Marvel? Did you find the jewel?'

'No,' Rags replied, 'but we did find this.'

Bags produced the note they had found under the stone. Nelly moved to take it, but Bags reached past her and gave it to Georgiana.

'Thank you, my dear,' the ghost said, as she unfolded it. 'Another clue. Now let me see.' She looked at the page and then she said, 'Maybe I don't need to read this one aloud.'

'Of course you do,' Nelly insisted. 'Go on, what is it?' Still Georgiana hesitated, but then she read from the page in her hand in a voice that wasn't quite steady:

'"Seek where your heart's love lies."'

'Gosh, that's a tricky one, isn't it?' Nelly said. 'I suppose everybody's got a different heart's love, and so they would all seek in different places.'

'Well, I wrote the note, so I know the answer

121

to this one,' Georgiana replied briskly. 'Now listen carefully, please,' she said to the rats, who noticed that she had gone quite pink. 'Do you know that old ivy-covered wall, around the kitchen garden?' Rags and Bags nodded. 'And the wooden door in it that opens into the garden? Just to the right of that, there's a little letterbox, sunk in the wall. It's not very easy to see because of all the ivy, but according to this note, that's where the next clue must be hidden. Will you go and find it? You *are* good boys!' she said, as the rats nodded again.

'So your heart's love . . .' the bat began, but Georgiana quickly interrupted her, saying rather sharply, 'That's quite enough for now, Nelly, thank you very much.'

'We'll go tomorrow,' Rags said, 'we promise.'

'And we'll bring whatever we find to you tomorrow night,' Bags added.

'Thank you so much, my dears. I'll see you then, same place, same time. Goodnight!'

And it was only when she stood up, walked

straight through the wall and disappeared, that the rats realised that they had completely forgotten to tell her about the young man they had seen in the garden, who had the same strange and rather alarming habit.

An Invitation from Nelly

'So what are you going to do now?' Rags asked the bat.

'Go home, I suppose.'

'What do you mean? Aren't you already there? Isn't Haverford-Snuffley Hall your home?'

'Yes,' said Nelly, 'but I mean *really* home. You know, home-home.'

The rats didn't know. As I have already told you, Rags and Bags had been born and grown up in a prison, and they'd got out of it as soon as they'd had the chance, even though it meant being stuck with a scoundrel like Jasper.

This meant that they found it hard to know what home was, let alone what the bat called a home-home. And then Nelly said, quite unexpectedly, 'Do you want to come with me?'

'That might be nice. But is it far from here?'

'Not at all. And now's a good time to go, because we'll be just in time for dinner.'

And that, of course, settled the matter.

Off they went, with the two rats scampering up the stairs and the bat flying ahead of them, to perch on a picture frame or a chair until such time as they caught up, and then leading the way again. Up and up they went, taking particular care to be quiet when they came to the door of Jasper's room, where they were relieved to hear him snoring. They kept on going until the stairs were narrow and the ceilings low and they were right up in the attics of Haverford-Snuffley Hall. I suppose it wasn't really a great distance from Georgiana's room, but scampering can be tiring, and the rats had already covered a lot of ground that day. They had even been swimming for the first time. They were worn out and hungry now, and it was a great relief when they came to a door and Nelly finally said, 'Here we are.' And then she called, 'Yoo-hoo! Hello! It's only me! Me and two friends.'

The door swung open and . . . what a sight met their eyes!

Bats! More bats than you could ever imagine gathered together in the one place. Old bats and baby bats. Plump bats and skinny bats. Cheerful bats, dozy bats, smart bats and silly bats. Bats! Bats! Bats! Dozens and dozens of them hanging in rows from racks on the ceiling.

And as if this wasn't a weird enough sight in itself, every single one of them was wearing some kind of hat. There was an old grey bat in a cloth cap, a very small bat in a knitted bonnet, a natty-looking bat in a top hat and another smart creature in a straw boater. And yes, Rags and Bags realised with dismay, there was an enormous, scary-looking bat with a woolly bobble hat pulled tightly over its head.

'Well, well,' said the bat, as Rags's and Bags's knees began to knock. 'Look what the wind blew in.'

'Oh, don't be a tease, Benny,' Nelly said. 'These are my friends.'

'Behaving themselves, are they?'

'Oh we are, we are!' the rats cried. 'We're really good these days. We're no trouble at all.'

'I'm glad to hear it,' Benny replied. 'Any friend of Nelly's is a friend of ours. We were just about to have dinner. Would you like to join us?'

'Of course they would,' Nelly said, replying for the rats. 'Ooh yum-yum, I'm so hungry. What's on the menu tonight?'

'We'll soon see.' And with that, Benny flew off to the far side of the room, with a single flap of his great wings.

Rags and Bags now realised that there was a dumb-waiter in this room too, as *PING!* Benny pressed a button and the metal doors slid open. Delicious smells of meat and of hot tomatoes and cheese filled the attic. 'We'll soon get this served up,' Benny said. 'Jim, come here and help me, there's a good lad.' A bat in a beret made of red felt swooped over and got right into the dumb-waiter. 'Ready? When I say three. One . . . two . . . three!'

Imagine a string of fairy lights, or a Christmas garland. And now try to imagine that, instead of light bulbs, or gold and silver stars, at intervals along the cord there are pizzas. Yes, pizzas. Tiny ones, crispy and scrumptious. And now imagine another garland, hung with little sausages; then another with chunks of cheese, another with green and red grapes, and finally, a garland of cakes, each one no bigger than a postage stamp, but each one iced and decorated. Benny and Jim took each of these marvels in turn out of the dumb-waiter and hung them from hooks, festooning the room until the whole place really did look as though it was decorated for Christmas, but with the strangest (and most delicious) baubles you ever saw.

'Tuck in, everybody! Enjoy your meal.'

But how were Rags and Bags to manage? All the food was hanging high above their heads, and they couldn't fly. They needn't have worried. All the bats took it in turn to throw things down to them.

'Here's a sausage! Catch!'

'Want some grapes? Red or green?' Pizzas whizzed down like edible Frisbees, fairy cakes dropped neatly into their waiting paws.

'I had no idea that that is the kind of food bats eat,' Rags said.

'It isn't really,' Nelly admitted. 'It's rather unusual. I suppose Mrs Haverford-Snuffley does spoil us a bit, and then Mrs Knuttmegg is such a good cook.'

'She's a star, our Mrs Haverford-Snuffley,' Benny said. 'She came into some money a few years ago and the very first thing she did was to fix up our attic, even before she got her own rooms sorted out. Put in central heating for us, got these racks installed for us to hang from, and worked out a system for the food, with hooks to hang it from. Thought of everything, she did.'

'You should have seen the state of the place before that,' Jim added. 'Holes in the roof, rain coming in, and talk about chilly. Awful, it was.'

'Nelly's too small to remember it, aren't you, Princess?' Benny said. 'All you've ever known is the lap of luxury, eh? That's my Princess!' Nelly smiled with pleasure at this, showing her sharp, pointed teeth. 'If ever we get the chance to pay Mrs Haverford-Snuffley back for all her kindness, we won't need to be asked twice, I can tell you that.'

'I suppose we should be going now,' Rags said, not wanting to overstay the welcome.

'Thank you for everything,' Bags added. 'It's been the most lovely evening, and the dinner was delicious.'

'How polite!' said a bat in a blue felt hat with

a green ribbon on it. 'What nicely mannered and well behaved rats! Who'd have expected such a thing?'

Getting home was no trouble at all. Rags and Bags climbed into the empty dumb-waiter, and waved goodbye to all their new friends.

'Thank you so much.'

'Our pleasure. Come again soon.'

'Goodbye.'

'See you tomorrow!' Nelly cried.

'Goodbye, goodbye.'

And with that, *PING!* the metal doors of the dumb-waiter slid closed, and the rats began their descent to Jasper's room.

Mrs Knutmegg and the Carrots

The following morning as Jasper was heading out to the garden, he met Mrs Knuttmegg at the bottom of the stairs.

'I need some vegetables from the kitchen garden,' she said. 'Six carrots. I'll be out to fetch them later and I'd ask you to be good enough to have them ready for me.'

Jasper flounced out of the house without even bothering to answer her, but after the business with flicking Mrs Haverford-Snuffley on the nose, he was keen not to get into any more trouble.

The kitchen garden was a charming spot.

It had a herb garden that scented the air when you walked past it and brushed against the leaves. There were fruit bushes, including blackcurrants and gooseberries. There were strawberry beds too, and raspberry canes. The vegetables grew in neat rows: lettuce and cabbage; leeks, and peas and beans.

But as Jasper stood that morning gazing over the garden he couldn't for the life of him work out where the carrots might be. Was there a carrot bush somewhere around that he hadn't noticed? He poked at some spinach with his toe. Maybe that was a carrot plant and they just weren't ready yet.

He still hadn't worked it out when Mrs Knuttmegg appeared at his elbow, skinny and stern in her dazzling white pinny.

'I've come for my veggies, mister.'

'I haven't got round to that yet. I had lots of other things to do.'

Mrs Knutmegg folded her arms. 'I'm in no rush,' she said. 'I'll wait here while you get them.'

'Wouldn't you like to get them yourself?'

'You're the gardener, that's your job.'

'Wouldn't you rather have a lettuce?'

'Mrs Haverford-Snuffley asked me to make carrot soup for her lunch. I need six carrots.'

Jasper looked around the garden wildly. 'I'm not sure that there are any here. I think the last gardener was really stupid and planted them in the wrong place. Do you know, now I come to think of it, I'm sure I saw a carrot bush down in the rose garden. Couldn't believe my eyes. What's that doing there? I asked myself. Covered in carrots it was though, oh yes, hundreds of them. Lovely and straight and a nice bright orange colour. Why don't you go down there and pick as many of them as you want. You see, I am rather busy here . . .'

'HA!' And Mrs Knuttmegg once again interrupted him with one of her harsh barks of laughter. Then she did something that astonished Jasper. She bent down and grasped a delicate feathery plant that was growing at her feet. She pulled hard on it and it came out of the ground . . . and there was a carrot! A nice fat pointy orange carrot!

'How did that get there?' Jasper said. 'I know – you put it there! You nasty, weird woman, hiding vegetables in the ground like that! What's wrong with you? What are you up to?'

Mrs Knuttmegg dropped the carrot and grabbed Jasper by his lapels, pulled his face up close to hers.

'It's not me, it's you,' she hissed. 'What are *you* up to, Professor Orchid? If that's your real name and you really are a gardener, I'll eat my biggest saucepan, and I'll have three tea-towels for dessert.'

She let go of Jasper's jacket and held her hands up close to his face. 'See these?'

Jasper could see nothing else. They were big hands, muscular and strong from years of kneading dough and mixing cakes. They were rough and red, and scarred from where she had cut herself when chopping things and where she had burnt herself on the kitchen stove when lifting things out of the oven.

'That's what a cook's mitts look like, mister,' she said proudly. Then she grabbed Jasper by the wrists and held him tightly so that he couldn't wriggle out of her grasp. She lifted his hands up to eye level so that they could both inspect them.

Jasper had beautiful hands. They were soft and white with not a mark on them. His fingernails were short, and perfectly clean. 'So you're telling me, mister,' she cried, 'that those are gardener's hands? That you've been digging and planting and weeding with these lily-white paws for years on end? Potting things? Pruning? Planting bulbs? Don't make me laugh.' But she did laugh: 'HA!'

Jasper knew he'd been rumbled.

Mrs Knuttmegg let go of his wrists and grabbed him by his jacket again. 'Let me tell you this about Mrs Haverford-Snuffley. There's not a kinder, more gentle and generous soul in all the world. She took me in when I was down on my luck, when I had nothing. I couldn't begin to tell you how good she's been to me. She's kind to dumb animals too. And because of all that, see, I watch out for her. If she has a fault it's that she can be too trusting, too nice. She doesn't know a villain when she sees one. She thinks everybody's as sweet and thoughtful as she is herself. But I'm not like that, oh no!'

'I didn't think you were,' Jasper said brazenly. 'As soon as I met you I knew you were a tough, suspicious old biddy who could see only the bad in people.'

'And there's plenty of bad to see in you,' Mrs Knuttmegg shot back immediately. 'If I knew what you were up to, I'd have you run out of here tomorrow.' She let go of his jacket again.

'I'm going back to my kitchen now,' she said, 'but I'll be keeping a close eye on you, mister. I'll be watching every move you make.' She bent down and picked up the carrot she had dropped earlier, then swiftly hauled five more out of the ground.

'Gardener, indeed,' she said as she shook the soil from the vegetables. 'Doesn't even know what a compost heap is. Carrot bush. HA!'

And with that she turned her back on Jasper and stumped off towards the house again.

23

Sing Your Heart Out!

While all of this was happening, Rags and Bags had sneaked off again, and were well on their way down the garden even before Mrs Knuttmegg had grabbed Jasper by his jacket.

'Well, here's the wall Georgiana talked about,' Rags said.

'And here's the wooden door. But where's the letterbox? I don't see it.'

'It must be hidden under all that ivy. I bet there wasn't as much of it in Georgiana's day.'

They decided that one of them would climb up and look for the letterbox while the other one stayed on the ground, and they were talking about this when Rags suddenly heard something. It was the distant notes of a flute.

'Oh no! It's that music again!' The sad, melancholy air grew louder and louder, and once again the rats began to feel very unhappy.

'I can't bear this, I don't want it,' Rags cried. 'What shall we do?'

'We'll sing a happy song,' Bags wailed miserably. 'Drown it out.'

'Do we know any happy songs?' asked Rags, who was already beginning to sob.

'"Happy Birthday." What about that?' Even in jail, all the prisoners would always sing for a birthday boy, and so Rags and Bags knew this song well.

'That's a good idea,' said Rags, who was weeping now, and full of a terrible grief. 'But who will we sing it for? Whose name will we put in?'

'Georgiana's,' Bags replied, as the tears rolled down his snout. The sad music was very loud and close now, as if the flute player was perhaps standing only on the other side of the wall. 'Join in with me, Rags, and be as loud and as cheerful as you can. Sing your heart out! One . . . two . . . three . . .'

'HAPPY BIRTHDAY TO YOU!
'HAPPY BIRTHDAY TO YOU!
'HAPPY BIRTHDAY GEORGIANA!
'HAPPY BIRTHDAY TO YOU!'

And with that, the most extraordinary thing happened.

The music stopped!

It stopped immediately, all at once, in the middle of the melody, as if someone had snatched the flute away. The rats were amazed.

'I didn't think that was going to happen,' Rags said, still shaken, and gulping away the last of his tears.

'It certainly did the trick,' Bags agreed, wiping his nose with the back of his paw and sniffing.

Gradually they started to recover and feel better again. They quickly decided that Rags would be the one to climb up the ivy and look for the letterbox. Rats are very good at climbing, and once he set out, he moved swiftly up the wall, while Bags watched from below.

'I've found it!' Rags shouted down. 'There's a hole in the wall here, a narrow rectangular hole. I'm going to climb in and see what's there.' His head, then his body, then his bum and finally his tail disappeared into the ivy-covered wall and Bags wondered excitedly what Rags would find. Might it even be the Green Marvel itself?

After what seemed to him to be hours, but was only a matter of minutes, a whiskered snout popped out, high up in the ivy.

'There are two notes this time. Which one should I bring?'

'Both of them, you twit! Throw them down to me here and I'll look after them.'

The snout disappeared again, and a few

seconds later a paw appeared, holding two folded squares of fragile yellowed paper which it tossed down. Bags caught them neatly, and before long Rags climbed out of the letterbox and was descending through the shiny green leaves of the ivy.

'We'll take these to Georgiana tonight and see what they say, but when we get back to the house I vote that we have a little snooze for a while,' Bags said.

'Good idea! I'm exhausted. That was almost too much excitement for one day!'

24

A Surprise for Jasper

When he had finished working that day, Jasper stumped upstairs to his room, feeling tired and irritated. It was early evening by then and already there was a full moon, low and huge and silvery. Jasper noticed it, but he paid it no heed, it meant nothing to him. Jasper only valued things that other people valued because they couldn't have them. For that reason he had no interest in wild flowers or birds or the stars or any of the other beautiful things in the world which are there for everyone to enjoy.

His body was aching from all the weeding and hoeing. He'd always known that Mrs

Knuttmegg didn't like or trust him, but he didn't like to be told it to his face. Oh, if only he could find the Green Marvel and leave this house, with its dotty owner and its nasty cook. For how much longer will I have to put up with all of this? he wondered.

And what about those miserable rats? They were more trouble than they were worth, as far as Jasper was concerned, but when he did finally leave he was going to take them with him. Even in jail rats were useful to frighten other prisoners, and although he would be rich and powerful once he found the necklace, he would still want to be able to scare the pants off people. What annoyed him here was that he had no way of controlling the wretched creatures. As soon as he had money, one of the very first things he was going to buy was a cage to keep them in. He'd go back to feeding them very little too. Be harsh and show them who's boss: that was the best way to treat animals as far as Jasper was concerned. Where were they, anyway? What were they doing right now? He stood listening carefully, and heard a little snore coming from the dressing table.

He crossed the room on tiptoe, gently pulled out the top drawer and there were the rats. They were both tucked up in their sock sleeping-bags, with their heads resting on the rolled-up vest. They seemed to be smiling in their sleep, and Jasper could see their tiny fangs. Ugh, what hideously ugly creatures they were, with their dull fur and weird little ears.

But then, as he looked at them with extreme dislike, Jasper noticed something. They were lying with their front paws out over the tops of the socks, and each rat was clutching a small square of folded paper. What's all this about? he wondered.

Carefully, very, very carefully so as not to waken them, with the tips of his fingers he gently removed the paper from the rat nearest to him, unfolded it and read it. 'What piffle!' he muttered to himself and he frowned. He didn't understand what the note was all about, but as far as he was concerned it was a pile of sentimental twaddle. With remarkable skill, he tucked the note back into the grip of the sleeping animal.

Was it even worth looking at the other one? It was probably more of the same codswallop. But Jasper was a born nosy-parker, and couldn't resist taking the second note too. As he did so, Rags – or was it Bags? He still found it hard to tell them apart and he wasn't interested enough in them to care which was which – as he did so, the rat yawned and stretched. For a moment he thought it was going to wake up, but it seemed instead to sink back into a deeper sleep, as he deftly removed the note from its little paws.

He unfolded it and glanced over it . . . and then he gasped. He read it again and then again. For a moment he thought he was going to faint, so astonished was he by what was written in the note. Jasper's hand was shaking with excitement when he put the piece of paper back in the rat's paws, and gently slid the drawer shut again.

Georgiana Is Upset

'Two notes? That's odd,' Georgiana said.

'One was lying in the bottom of the letterbox,' Rags replied, 'and the other was up at the top, stuck in between the wood of the box and the wall itself. It was as if someone had posted it but instead of it dropping down as normal, it got stuck at the top.'

'That's odd,' Georgiana said again.

They had all gathered in her room once more. Tonight it was quite brightly lit, because of the full moon shining and because of Georgiana's own natural luminosity. She took the first note and unfolded it very carefully because the paper was so old and fragile. 'Read it aloud please,' said Nelly.

'My darl—' Georgiana began, and then a look of surprise crossed her face. She said no more, but read the note silently to herself. The three animals watched her closely and saw her surprise change to dismay. 'Oh no!' she said at last. 'This is terrible! Terrible!' Tears welled up in her big green eyes and she started to cry.

What a racket she made! 'BOO HOO HOO! WAAAAHH!' Her wailing echoed around the room and grew louder as it bounced off the walls. Rags and Bags put their paws over their ears to block out the frightful noise. 'WOOOOH! WAAAAHHH! BOO HOO HOO!'

'Don't, please, poor Georgiana,' Nelly cried, fluttering around her head and trying to console her. 'What's the matter? Why are you upset?'

'It's this,' said Georgiana, picking up the note and shaking it. 'It's terrible.'

'What does it say?' Nelly asked.

'I don't know if I can read it to you, it's too upsetting.'

'Oh go on! You have to tell us!'

The rats had sometimes thought that, although they liked the bat, it could be a nosy little creature, and they thought so now.

'If I must, then,' Georgiana said and she sighed, wiping the tears away from her extraordinary green eyes, and she smoothed out the note on her knee.

'"My darling Georgiana,

'"Be in the folly at midnight tonight. I will be there with two horses. I am more happy and excited than I can ever tell you. Soon we will be together forever. I love you with all my heart." And then there are three kisses. BOO HOO HOO!'

Her voice had gone all strange and weepy the more she read, and by the time she got to the end of the message she was wailing again. But the animals were still mystified. Why should such an affectionate note make her so unhappy? And what had horses got to do with anything? What did it all mean?

Bags pointed at the clock. 'If you're to be at the folly by midnight, you should leave now,' he said, 'or else you're going to be late.'

'But I'm already too late! Two hundred years too late!'

'Georgiana, we don't understand any of this,' Rags said.

'Very well then,' she said, still holding the note tightly, 'let me explain.'

26

Toby

'I told you,' she began, 'about the man who gave me the emerald necklace because it was the same colour as my eyes, and about how he wanted to marry me.'

'But you wouldn't,' Nelly said.

'Because he was vain and proud,' Bags added.

'That's right,' said Georgiana. 'You've remembered the story well. My parents were cross with me, because they thought I should marry for money, and that whether or not I loved the man didn't matter. But to me, that was a horrible idea.

153

'What I didn't tell you,' she went on, 'was that shortly after that someone else also gave me a present. It was the boy who worked in the garden, here at the Hall. His name was Toby, and he gave me a red squirrel. He knew what had happened and he said he couldn't buy me emeralds to match the colour of my eyes, because he had no money, so he caught and tamed a squirrel for me to keep as a pet. He said its fur was the same colour as my hair,' and she shook her glossy red curls proudly as she said this.

'It was the most endearing creature. It used to fall asleep in my arms, and when it awoke I fed it hazelnuts. I used to take it down to the folly when I went there to meet Toby. My parents were completely against my having anything to do with him because he worked in the garden and he wasn't rich. It was so foolish of them. What really mattered was that he was the sweetest, kindest, most gentle man you could imagine. We used to have to meet in secret. We'd leave little notes for each other in the letterbox, and then I'd sneak off and see him in the folly, at whatever time we had agreed. He used to play music for me there on the flute.'

When she said this, the rats looked at each other.

'Sad music?' Rags asked.

'Why no, not at all,' she replied. 'It was the happiest, most joyful music. Even if you were feeling a little bit gloomy and glum, as soon as he started to play your spirit would lift and your heart would be flooded with joy. Oh, it was the sweetest music ever, as pure and delightful as the song of a bird. Those were the happiest moments of my life, sitting in the folly with the squirrel asleep in my arms, so soft and warm, while Toby played the flute.'

'Did Toby have fair hair?' Bags asked.

'Yes,' Georgiana replied absently, 'cut in a square fringe. And I always thought his work clothes looked so nice, so soft and brown.'

Again the two rats looked at each other.

'Oh, I loved him so much!' Georgiana suddenly cried. 'And when he asked me to marry him, of course I said yes. I knew my parents would never agree and so we decided to elope.'

'What does that mean?' Nelly asked.

'It means running away together to get married in secret.'

'Ooh, how romantic and exciting!' the little bat gasped.

'Toby said he would leave a note for me in the letterbox, arranging a time. It was to be on a night such as this,' and she nodded towards the window, 'the night of a full moon. Well, I waited and waited and waited. I checked the box again and again, but there was no message. Toby and I never got married, and I never married anyone else. No one would have wanted me after that, because I became the saddest girl in the world. I couldn't understand it, because I knew Toby loved me with all his heart. He had promised he would leave me a note and he always kept his promises.'

'And he did,' Nelly said soothingly. 'He did love you and he did leave you a note arranging to elope with you, just like he said he would.'

'But it got stuck in the box and I never found it. He must have waited in the moonlight with the horses for hours for me. He must have thought that I had let him down, that I had changed my mind and decided not to marry him after all. Oh, it's so upsetting to think of that. It's terrible, I can't bear it!'

Her eyes were filling up with tears again. To distract her Bags asked quickly, 'And what about the squirrel? What happened to it?'

Georgiana's face crumpled up and went red.

'It ran away!' she wailed. 'The squirrel ran away, back into the woodland, and I never saw it again. BOO HOO HOO!'

And she started to cry again, much to the dismay of the animals, who hated the sound of her wailing.

'There, there,' said Rags, 'don't be so upset.'

'Look, you're forgetting about the other note,' Nelly said, partly to give Georgiana something else to think about, and partly out of curiosity. 'We still don't know what that says.'

'We'd better take a look at it, I suppose,' the ghost said, sniffing and wiping her eyes. She picked up the little square of paper and unfolded it, smoothed it out on her knee. 'I can't imagine that it will be anything too exciting. It's in my handwriting anyway, I can see that.'

'It'll be another clue about the Green Marvel. Time to get our thinking caps on,' Bags said.

But it wasn't a clue. It was something absolutely amazing, something none of them had expected, and when Georgiana read it for them they all gasped out loud.

27

Treasure Seekers

'The Green Marvel is hidden in the kitchen. Press the third tile to the left of the window hard three times and it will open a secret compartment. There is a small metal box in the compartment, and the Green Marvel is inside the metal box.'

They all sat there for a few moments, too stunned to speak. Could it really be as simple as that? Had it truly been in the kitchen all that time without anyone knowing? Georgiana seemed to think so, for once she got over her surprise she gave a little whoop of delight.

'So off we go to the kitchen then, to find my necklace!'

They all left the room together, and made their way swiftly through the dark and silent house. Georgiana swept down the main staircase with the rats at her heels, trying their best not to get tangled in the hem of her billowing silk dress. Nelly fluttered along beside them. 'This is so exciting!' the little bat cried. 'I thought things like this only ever happened in books.'

On and on they went, until finally they came to the kitchen door. They could see that there was a light on, but the rats knew from their last visit that Mrs Knuttmegg usually left a lamp burning throughout the night, so they thought nothing of it. They all crowded round Georgiana as she pushed the door open . . . and immediately they all got the shock of their lives!

There was Jasper. He was standing at the far side of the room and had his back to them, but he heard the door opening and turned around to see who it was. As he did so, Georgiana walked straight through a cupboard and out the other side of it. From where she stood now in the shadows she could still see Jasper clearly. The rats slipped under a meat safe and Nelly roosted high up on a dresser, quite terrified, and hoping she wouldn't be seen.

It was a near thing, but they were quick off the mark, and while Jasper heard strange noises – a rustle like silk, a scampering, scratching sound and a flutter high up in the room – he didn't know what to make of it all, and he saw absolutely nothing.

'Hmm, must be a draught,' he muttered to himself, and he turned back to what he was doing.

Georgiana and the animals watched in dismay.

'Now let me see . . . third tile to the left.' He pressed it hard three times and the tile popped open. 'So far, so good,' Jasper said, as he put his hand into the hole in the wall. Holding his breath, he lifted out a little metal box, turned around and placed it on the kitchen table. Slowly and carefully he opened it, lifted something out of it and held it up in the lamplight.

As he did so, there was a little yelp from the side of the cupboard, a gasp from the top of the dresser and two shrill squeaks from under the meat safe. But Jasper heard none of this. At that precise moment a brass band could have played the national anthem loud in his ear and followed it up with a party song as an encore and still Jasper would have heard nothing. He was completely absorbed and fascinated by what he had found.

And to tell the truth, who could blame him? For there, in his trembling hands, was a necklace. Oh, but such a necklace! It was made of emeralds set in gold, and all the stones were huge. There were square ones, and some were cut in the shape of a pear. Right in the middle was a rectangular stone, so enormous that it was impossible to imagine that anywhere in the world there might be a bigger emerald.

The beauty of those jewels, how can I describe them? They were a deep green colour: as green as a fresh bright leaf, as green as the ocean in a hidden cove, as green, yes indeed, as green as Georgiana's extraordinary eyes. The emeralds glittered and sparkled in the light of the lamp.

So this was it.

This was the Green Marvel.

Jasper gave a little groan of selfishness and greed. 'Mine,' he murmured. 'All mine.'

But just with that, something completely unexpected happened.

Jasper Shows His True Colours

'Professor Orchid!'

While Jasper had been gazing at the necklace, Mrs Haverford–Snuffley and Mrs Knuttmegg, both in dressing gowns and hairnets, had come into the kitchen. 'Why, Professor, what on earth are you doing here in the middle of the night?'

'He's got the necklace, look,' Mrs Knuttmegg cried. 'He's got the Green Marvel!'

'It's mine, not yours,' Jasper said, dropping it into his pocket, 'and you're not getting it, so don't even bother thinking about it.'

'He's a bad egg, missus. I knew it as soon

as I clapped eyes on him. I knew he wasn't a gardener.'

'What are you talking about, Mrs Knuttmegg? Not a gardener? What can you possibly mean?'

'The nasty old biddy is correct,' Jasper replied. 'Smart fellow like me waste my life on flowers and vegetables? No chance!'

Mrs Haverford-Snuffley looked shocked and bewildered. 'I don't understand,' she said. 'Can this really be true?'

Jasper gave a horrible grin and nodded.

'So . . . so you don't know anything at all about plants and gardens?'

'Not a thing,' Jasper said proudly.

'He's been lying to you all along, missus.'

'And so your name isn't really Professor Orchid?'

'Nope.'

The elderly lady stood there in the soft light of the lamp, looking confused and bewildered. 'Can this really be true?' she said again.

Suddenly an awful thought crossed her mind.

'If you lied about the gardening, did you lie to me about other things too? Is it possible then that you lied about—' and her voice fell to a whisper, for she could hardly bring herself to speak the words. 'Is it possible that you don't really . . . like . . . bats?'

'Bats?' Jasper said. 'Bats? With their nasty red mouths and pointy teeth? Their horrid fur and their hideous bony wings? No, you mad old sausage, I don't like bats. I HATE them! Yuk! Urg! They make my flesh crawl.'

Mrs Haverford-Snuffley gasped and put her hand over her mouth.

'Can this be true? But you must like Mummy's little sweetheart?' Her voice was pleading now. 'My own little possum? What about my cutie-pie, adorable little baby-waby batty-watty?'

'I hate it above all!' Jasper shouted. 'It's the worst! It's my least favourite bat in the whole wide world!'

Mrs Haverford-Snuffley gave a low moan,

and then she started to cry. Mrs Knuttmegg put her arms around the old lady and hugged her.

'There, there, missus, don't pay him any heed. He's an evil, wicked man. And you are, too,' she shouted at Jasper. 'You're badness itself. And that necklace you've got, you've no right to it. It belongs to missus, because it was in her house.'

'Well, it's mine now and there's nothing anybody can do about it.' He snatched up a rolling pin that was sitting on a nearby work-top, and he waved it menacingly. 'Any more of your lip and you'll be sorry.'

'Threaten me with my own rolling pin? How dare you?'

'I'll do better than that,' Jasper said, and in no time at all he had tied Mrs Knuttmegg's hands behind her back, using one of her own tea-towels.

'You villain! You'll pay for this,' she shouted as she wriggled and struggled.

'Who's going to make me?' Jasper sneered as he double-knotted the tea-towel. When he had finished with Mrs Knuttmegg he tied up Mrs Haverford-Snuffley, who didn't struggle at all because she was so frightened.

'I'm the boss now,' Jasper said, picking up the rolling pin again. 'You have to do whatever I say. Now move!'

He pushed the two women out into the hallway, and opened the back door. Poking at them with the rolling pin, he then forced them out into the night.

 **29**

To the Rescue!

As soon as Jasper and the two women had left the house, Georgiana came out from the side of the cupboard and rushed over to the window.

'He's taking them through the garden,' she cried. 'Oh, the poor things!'

'Go after them, Georgiana,' Nelly said. 'See exactly where they go. We'll follow you as soon as we can.'

Georgiana stared at her blankly. 'Me? You want me to go out into the garden? I can't possibly do that.'

'But you must,' Nelly cried, dismayed.

'After the night I was supposed to elope with

169

Toby, I never went out of the house ever again,' Georgiana said. 'It was too sad, I couldn't bear it.' She looked frightened and anxious now. 'I haven't been in the garden for over two hundred years!'

'But you must,' Nelly said again. 'We have to save those two nice women from that horrible man. Please, Georgiana, please help us.'

The ghost took a deep breath, and without another word she walked through the kitchen wall and disappeared.

'What are we going to do, Nelly?' Rags asked.

'We're going to get help. Follow me.' She fluttered into the dumb-waiter and the rats climbed in beside her. 'Press the button please, Bags.' *PING!* The steel doors closed and the dumb-waiter started to ascend.

When the doors opened again, the animals found themselves gazing into the dining room. 'This isn't where we want to be,' Nelly said crossly. 'Push the button again please, Bags.'

PING! This time the dumb-waiter started to descend and Nelly gave a loud squeak of impatience. 'These things never work the way you want them to. Oh, this is so annoying!' For the doors had opened again and they found themselves once more back in the kitchen.

'We'll give it one last try.' This time Nelly herself got out and hammered on the button of the dumb-waiter. *PING! PING! PING!* Now they were going up again, up and up and up, until finally they lurched to a halt. 'This had better be the right place,' Nelly muttered as the metal doors slid back.

'Hello, Princess! What kept you? You're late for your dinner.' It was Benny speaking, for they were back in the attic where all the bats lived. 'Oh, hello, you two,' he went on, for he had suddenly noticed Rags and Bags. 'Nelly, you should have told us you'd be bringing your two friends with you tonight.'

'Oh, Benny,' Nelly gasped, 'something terrible has happened.' As she quickly told the whole of their night's adventure so far, the two rats gazed up at the rows and rows of bats on their roosts. All of them were listening intently to what Nelly said.

'This will never do,' Benny cried when she had finished. 'We'll have to stop that rascal and save those poor ladies.'

'I'll lead the way,' Nelly said.

'And we'll follow!' the big bat shouted in reply. But then suddenly he remembered Rags and Bags. He stared at them for a few moments.

'Hmmn, we can't leave you here, can we? Jim, will you help me with this?'

The bat in the felt beret, who Rags and Bags remembered had helped to serve the food the last time, nodded his head. Benny and Jim swooped down to where the two nervous rats were sitting on the floor. 'Climb aboard,' Benny said, turning his back on Bags.

'What . . . what do you mean?'

'I'm going to give you a piggy-back. You know, a lift.'

'That's awfully kind, but I think . . .' Bags stammered.

'We couldn't possibly put you to such trouble,' Rags quickly added.

'Didn't you tell us the last time that you can't fly?' Jim said sternly.

The rats nodded their heads. 'In that case, stop talking twaddle and hop up there. We have no time at all to lose.'

There was nothing else for it. Timidly, the two rats each climbed on to the back of a bat. It felt very odd.

'Hold on tight.'

'Oh we will! We will!'

'Aaargh, not that tight! You're choking me,' Jim gasped.

'Sorry,' Rags said, and he loosened the grip of his paws around Jim's neck.

'Just be sure not to fall off. Everybody ready now? Are we all set?'

'YES!' the bats cried aloud.

'Then we're off. Little 'uns first. Nelly, lead the way!'

30

Whoosh!

Followed by a stream of the smallest bats, Nelly fluttered over to the fireplace on the far side of the room and, to the astonishment of the rats, flew straight up the chimney.

'Go! Go! Go!' Benny cried as all the others followed on, every last one of them, even the babies and the grannies. Their flapping wings made a cold wind in the attic, and there was a loud humming noise. It was all incredibly well organised, with no bumping, no pushing or shoving. Two by two all the bats flew across the room and disappeared into the fireplace, with Benny and Jim the last to go.

'To the rescue! Geronimo!'

The next thing Rags and Bags knew, they were being carried across the attic in swift, juddering flight on the bats' backs. For one horrible moment they thought they were going to smash into the back of the fireplace, but just in time Benny and Jim skilfully changed direction and flew straight up. They were in a narrow brick tunnel now that smelt powerfully of soot and smoke. Oh, it was a horrible place! In spite of themselves the rats began to splutter and cough.

Maybe this is just a dream, Rags thought, and any moment now I'll wake up in my sock, with my head on the rolled-up vest and Bags asleep beside me. But in his heart he knew that it was all really happening.

If only we had never left prison! Bags said to himself, as he clung for dear life to the bat's neck. It wasn't such a bad place after all. But he knew deep down that this wasn't true.

Just when they thought they could stand it

no longer, WHOOSH! They shot out of the chimney pot and into the night sky. What a sight met their eyes!

They were at the end of a great line of bats, all flying two by two. The air was full of the sound of their wings. Flapping and fluttering, they flew across the full moon, and it seemed to the rats that if they were to stretch out their paws, they would be able to touch its silver face. Far, far below them they could see the roof of Haverford-Snuffley Hall. They could see the gardens, all the flower beds and the lawns, the kitchen garden and the greenhouses. They could see the lake in the distance and the island where the folly stood, and all of these things, with which they were so familiar, looked like toys now. Everything was laid out neatly and clearly as if it were on a map. Still they continued to soar.

Far ahead of them they could see Nelly, the only bat who was flying solo, bravely leading the way. Rags remembered the first time he had met her, and was ashamed to think how they had teased her and pinched her bonnet. What a mean, stupid thing to do!

Just at that very moment, Nelly dived straight down at speed. All the other bats followed her, zooming towards the ground. It was most unpleasant for Rags and Bags, who felt that they had left their tummies somewhere up near the moon, as the rest of their bodies hurtled downwards.

'Oooh, this is so weird,' Bags moaned, and he pressed his face into the back of Benny's neck.

'I'm going to be sick!' Rags wailed.

'Hold on tight and you'll be fine,' Jim yelled.

Down and down they went, as the ground raced up to meet them.

What had Nelly seen?

31

Shocks and Surprises for Everyone

While all of this was happening, Georgiana had been running through the gardens in the moonlight. How strange it was to be out in the cool night air, after being closed up in the house for more than two hundred years! I should have done this before now, she thought. I should have looked for Toby after that night and tried to find out what went wrong. Sometimes love lasts forever and Georgiana still loved Toby. She forced herself now to think about the job in hand. She had to stay near enough to Jasper and the women so as not to lose track of them, but not so close that they might see or hear her.

There was one tricky moment when she did draw too near, and Jasper heard the rustle of her billowing silk dress.

'What was that?' he said, stopping and looking back. Georgiana had no choice but to step into the trunk of an ancient oak and disappear.

'Hmm,' Jasper said, frowning. 'It must be the wind in the trees.' He turned back and gave Mrs Knuttmegg another poke with the rolling pin. 'Go on, keep moving.'

'You villain,' she said. Mrs Haverford-Snuffley was still sobbing, but more quietly now.

The little group continued on its way and Georgiana came out of the oak, feeling very peculiar. She had walked through things such as doors and walls on countless occasions, but this was the first time she had walked into a solid object and stayed in it, if only for a moment. It had been a peculiar feeling, both uncomfortable and unpleasant, and she hoped she wouldn't have to do it again.

She continued to tiptoe after the little group, and tried hard not to make a noise. Soon Georgiana was again close enough to hear what they were saying to each other.

'What are you going to do with us?' Mrs Haverford–Snuffley whimpered.

'I'm going to lock you up,' Jasper said. 'Then I'm going to go back to the house and pinch everything I want. That nice silver bowl in the hallway, for example, I've always fancied that. And I'm keeping the Green Marvel, of course. By the time you're found, I'll be far away, with all the goodies.'

'Don't think you'll get away with it,' Mrs Knuttmegg cried. In reply Jasper waved the rolling pin at her in a menacing way.

By this time they were at the back of the walled garden, near the compost heap. 'You're not going to lock us in the potting shed, are you?' cried Mrs Haverford–Snuffley.

'Just see if I don't.'

'But it's horrible in there. It's dark and it's full of spiders.'

'That's your problem, not mine,' Jasper said as he fumbled to unlock the door.

Oh, what am I going to do? Georgiana thought in despair. Where are Nelly and the rats? And then she remembered something enormously important: *I'm a ghost!*

Over the years Georgiana had often frightened people, but always accidentally. She would wander through walls into rooms that she thought were empty, only to find some unfortunate houseguest sitting on the bed in their underwear. People would come into her little room, where she was sitting on the sofa, and when she shyly melted away through the wall the sound of their screams would follow her for ages. But never had she deliberately set out to frighten anyone.

Not until tonight.

Taking a deep breath, she jumped out from

behind a tree, into full view of Jasper and the women. 'WOOOOH,' she cried, wishing that she had a chain to rattle, or that she could take her head off and put it under her arm. 'WOOOOH!'

But she didn't need any special effects. All three immediately recognised her from the painting in the hallway, and they knew at once that she was a . . .

'GHOST! AAARGH! GHOST! GHOST!' Even Jasper, who didn't believe in ghosts, was terrified. Georgiana was encouraged by their reaction. 'WOOOOH!'

High above them all, somewhere up near the moon, Nelly heard the commotion. Peering down, she saw what was happening and began her rapid descent. 'WOOOH!' Georgiana cried for a fourth time.

And then yet again something completely unexpected and amazing happened.

A second ghost walked straight through the garden wall and stood before them. It was a young man, with blond hair cut in a square fringe and he was dressed in soft brown clothes. Georgiana gave a loud scream of shock and delight.

'Toby!'

'Georgiana! I thought I heard your voice but I couldn't believe it. Is it you? Is it really you, my darling?'

But before she could reply, the air was filled with a strange humming and buzzing noise, growing stronger all the time, until it was incredibly loud. 'My bats!' Mrs Haverford-Snuffley shouted in delight. 'It's Mummy's little pumpkin! It's my wonderful little darling batty-watty and all her family!'

The great dark cloud of bats descended and swarmed Jasper.

'Eeek! Gerroff! Leave me alone!'

In all the hurly-burly he dropped the rolling pin, just as Mrs Knuttmegg, who had been wriggling ever since they left the house, struggled free from the tea-towel. She quickly untied her employer, and snatched up her rolling pin.

'Go and get help, missus,' she shouted. 'I'll deal with this rascal.'

Mrs Haverford–Snuffley scampered off in the direction of the Hall, while Jasper tried to run away.

But, baffled by bats, terrified of the ghosts and cornered by Mrs Knuttmegg, it was all too much for him. He stumbled and fell head first into the compost heap, in amongst all the rotting potato peelings and manky egg shells. The bats settled on him in a great pile, so that he couldn't beat them off.

And Jasper knew then that the game was up.

32

How the Night Ended

'So you're telling us there was a ghost,' said the policeman.

'Two ghosts,' said Mrs Haverford-Snuffley. 'You see, in the first place, we went to the kitchen in the middle of the night because of a ghost. We've always known the house was haunted, and not long after I went to bed I was woken by a terrible howling. Mrs Knuttmegg heard it too and so she came to see if I was all right. She very kindly offered to make me a cocoa to help me get back to sleep and we went down to the kitchen together, because we were both very afraid. But it was only in the garden that we saw the ghosts. Two of them,' she said again.

'And where are they now?' the policeman asked.

'I don't know. They just sort of disappeared.'

'Well, they would, I suppose, being ghosts,' the policeman said sarcastically.

'We've heard all this before,' the policewoman muttered. 'They'll be telling us next there was a rolling pin involved.'

'There was, actually,' Mrs Knuttmegg said. 'It belongs to me. That villain poked me and threatened me with my own rolling pin. Can you believe the cheek of it?'

They were all four gathered together in the drawing room of Haverford-Snuffley Hall. Mrs Knuttmegg and her employer were still in their night clothes, with Nelly now clinging to Mrs Haverford-Snuffley's hairnet. Through the big windows they could see that the sky was pale, for dawn was breaking.

'Well, it's all over now,' the policeman said.

'The main thing is that your jewels are safe,' and he nodded towards the table where the Green Marvel lay.

'Yes, thank you so much. This is such a wonderful surprise. To think that the necklace was in the kitchen all along! But tell me, are you sure that that bad man won't come back?'

'He's on his way to Woodford prison as we speak. They'll have to give him a jolly good wash when they get him there. Talk about a stink! Buried in a compost heap and covered in bats. Never in all my years in the force have I seen such a thing.'

'What happened to the bats?' Mrs Haverford-Snuffley asked anxiously.

'They flew away as soon as we got there,' the policewoman said. 'Went off in a big long line, two by two. Quite a sight it was. I might have been mistaken, but I thought they flew straight down one of the chimneys of this house. I'd see about that, if I was you, or else you'll have an attic full of bats. Before you know where you are, they'll have settled down and made themselves at home, and who would want that?'

Mrs Haverford-Snuffley and Mrs Knuttmegg said nothing in reply, but they looked at each other and grinned.

'Speaking of animals, that reminds me,' the policeman said. 'We found these two creatures at the scene of the crime. I don't know what we'll do with them. Horrible, they are.'

Gingerly he put his hand in the pocket of his jacket and pulled out . . . Rags and Bags.

'Just look at them!' he said in disgust, as he dumped them on the table beside the Green Marvel.

Mrs Haverford-Snuffley drew near and did just that. She looked at them for a long time, staring hard at their beady eyes and long tails, at their whiskers and their tatty fur.

'Rats,' she whispered. 'Two rats. Goodness me, why, aren't they just . . . ADORABLE!'

And to the astonishment of everyone else,

she swept them up in her arms and started to cuddle them. 'Snooky-ooky ratty-watties! Mummy's little cup-cakes! Who are the best little beasties in the whole wide world?'

I hope you don't imagine for a moment that Rags and Bags were annoyed or embarrassed at all this baby-talk. They were absolutely chuffed, and went pink with delight under their fur.

Suddenly Mrs Knuttmegg spoke. 'What's that noise? A kind of squeaking sound, do you hear it?'

It was Nelly, of course. She had never heard anything funnier in her whole life, and was laughing so much she almost fell off the hairnet.

 **33**

The End

When the Green Marvel was sold at auction in the Woodford Saleroom, it was possibly the most exciting day the town had ever seen. The place was packed with people, and they all gasped with amazement when the necklace was held up for them to see. Never could they have imagined such jewels! The auction started and the price just kept on getting higher and higher. When the auctioneer finally banged on the table and cried 'Sold!' everyone in the room gasped again, and some shouted and even cheered, for the Green Marvel had been sold for a truly mind-boggling sum of money.

Now Mrs Haverford-Snuffley would be able to fulfil her dream.

Work started at the Hall soon afterwards. Stables were built, together with sties and byres. Hutches were bought, kennels and a great many perches and baskets, together with troughs, and dishes, toys and blankets. Before the year was out, the whole town gathered again for the grand opening of the Haverford-Snuffley Hall Animal Sanctuary.

It has been running for quite some time now and is a tremendous success. There are all sorts of animals: hedgehogs and donkeys; puppies and pigs; foxes and kittens; hamsters and goats. People who can offer a good home go there to choose a pet, but a great many simply go to visit the animals and to spend a happy afternoon. It's the most charming place you can imagine and Mrs Haverford-Snuffley is immensely popular with everyone.

Mrs Knuttmegg has opened a tea-room for the visitors. She serves scones and apple pie and shortbread and pastries, all home-baked and all delicious. So many people asked her for her recipes that she eventually published *Mrs Knuttmegg's Big Book of Baking*, which stayed at the top of the bestseller lists for months, much to her surprise and delight. The follow-up, *Mrs Knuttmegg's Dynamite Book of Dinners*, is due in the bookshops any day now.

Haverford-Snuffley Hall is still haunted, but in a good way. Sometimes in the night, singing and laughter can be heard coming from empty rooms. On occasion people walking in the gardens hear music, pure and sweet as the song of a bird. And even if they are feeling a little bit gloomy at the time, they feel better as soon as they hear the music, and in no time at all their hearts are overflowing with joy and happiness. Others even claim to have seen a ghostly couple walking in the garden, smiling and holding hands. The young man is dressed in soft brown clothes and has blond hair cut in a square fringe. The young woman wears a billowing blue silk dress. She has white skin, a straight nose, and extraordinary green eyes. Her hair, which she wears piled up on the top of her head, is exactly the same beautiful red colour as the little squirrel that plays in the branches above their heads, and that the young woman sometimes coaxes down into her arms.

All the bats are still in the attic. Nelly is still hanging from a long feather on Mrs Haverford-Snuffley's hat. And what of Rags and Bags? Mrs Haverford-Snuffley has made pets of them, and carries them around with her everywhere she goes, in a small basket. She is on a one-woman mission to persuade people that rats are actually rather nice, and can even be very lovable. I'm afraid she isn't making much progress. People can be very fixed in their ideas, but no matter. Rags and Bags are well fed and well looked after. They have become healthy and plump and sleek, and are like brothers to Nelly. The rats couldn't be happier, and they are thrilled to have Jasper out of their lives.

And indeed, what about Jasper? Well, he's back in prison, safely under lock and key for a long spell. When he arrived, he sulked and huffed for ages. But he won't be in prison forever, and when he does get out I shouldn't be surprised if he's up to his old tricks again before long, making trouble and having all kinds of mad adventures. If that does happen, I'll write another book and tell you all about it.

But only if you promise to behave. Only if you're good.

The End